HARBINGERS 7

Infiltration

Angela Hunt

Alton Gansky, Bill Myers, and Frank Peretti

HARBINGERS

A novella series by

Bill Myers, Frank Peretti, Angela Hunt, and Alton Gansky

In this fast-paced world with all its demands, the four of us wanted to try something new. Instead of the longer novel format, we wanted to write something equally as engaging but that could be read in one or two sittings—on the plane, waiting to pick up the kids from soccer, or as an evening's read.

We also wanted to play. As friends and seasoned novelists, we thought it would be fun to create a game we could participate in together. The rules were simple:

Rule #1

Each of us would write as if we were one of the characters in the series:

Bill Myers would write as Brenda, the street-hustling tattoo artist who sees images of the future.

Frank Peretti would write as the professor, the atheist ex-priest ruled by logic.

Angela Hunt would write as Andi, the professor's brilliant-but-geeky assistant who sees inexplicable patterns.

Alton Gansky would write as Tank, the naïve, big-hearted jock with a surprising connection to a healing power.

Rule #2

Instead of the four of us writing one novella together (we're friends but not crazy), we would write it like a TV series. There would be an overarching story line into which we'd plug our individual novellas, with each story written from our character's point of view.

Bill's first novella, *The Call*, sets the stage. It was followed by Frank's, *The Haunted*, Angela's *The Sentinels*, and Alton's *The Girl*. And then began Cycle Two: *The Revealing, Infestation, Infiltration,* and ??

If we keep having fun, we'll begin a third round and so on until other demands pull us away or, as in TV, we get cancelled.

There you have it. We hope you'll find these as entertaining in the reading as we did in the writing.

Bill, Frank, Angie, and Al

Chapter 1

"What's that address again?" I asked Tank, who held the professor's note. "Was it 2468 Gulf?"

"Twenty-four sixty nine," he said, bending to peer out my window. "Probably that one right there."

I pulled into the narrow driveway and shut off the ignition, then surveyed the place the professor had rented.

"Cool beach cottage," Brenda said, opening the rear door. "Come on, Daniel my man. Let's see what the prof's been up to while we were packing."

I drew a deep breath and slowly released it in an effort to calm my pounding heart. Only two days ago our team— me, Brenda Barnick, Tank, and Professor McKinney— had been involved in a life-or-death struggle with green powder and flying orbs, and I wasn't exactly eager to go another round with whatever had confronted us. But the professor had been adamant about not stopping to lick our wounds. We had to go on the offensive, he kept saying, we had to stop reacting and start being proactive.

The thought didn't thrill me.

I got out, then went around to open the trunk. Anything to keep from rushing headlong into whatever the professor was planning.

I grabbed a couple of bags, then turned to survey the street. Gulf Boulevard snaked along the coast in this part of the county, so dozens of beach houses and condos here were available to rent. Still on an emotional high from our last escapade, the professor had rented this house for a month—but I sincerely hoped we wouldn't need it that long. I could handle an occasional adrenaline rush, but running with Brenda, Tank, Daniel, and the professor full time was enough to fry my circuits. After all, none of *them* had ended up in the hospital's behavioral unit, but I did. And though I'd been pronounced physically fit by my doctor, my emotions felt a little unsteady. And for good reason: I'd been only hours away from exploding like a bag of green powder.

"Andi?" Tank turned, his smile fading to a look of concern. "You okay?"

"I'm great." I plastered on a big, fake grin and trotted up the concrete porch steps.

Inside the house, Brenda and Professor McKinney were bent over the dining room table. I dropped my bags onto a functional sofa as Tank entered behind me. In no hurry to join the others, I turned to admire the not-so-admirable art on the walls. "Interesting place, don't you think?" I murmured, taking in the nondescript lamps, the mostly empty bookcase, and the stack of tattered magazines on the coffee table.

"All the comforts of home," Tank said. His gaze

wandered to the dining room, then shifted to Daniel, who sat on the couch, his hands empty and his gaze blank.

"That reminds me," I said, rummaging in my purse. "I picked up a little something for Daniel." I found the small box and handed it to him. "Here. I hope this will give you something to do while we're talking. Plus, if you ever get separated from us, you can give us a call."

Daniel's eyes went wide as he held the iPhone box. "For me?"

"For real and for you," I told him. "My provider has a package plan, so no big deal. I've already programed it with our names and numbers, e-mail addresses, all that. I'm sure Tank would be happy to recommend some really cool games, too."

Daniel opened the box and lifted out the phone with an almost-reverent look.

"I'll help you download some killer apps," Tank promised. "Soon as we've finished talking to the prof." He turned to me. "Don't you want to see what the professor's been up to?"

"I guess." I forced another smile and reluctantly followed Tank into the dining room. On the table, gleaming beneath a chandelier that might have been fashionable in the seventies, was an orb—a slave, we assumed, of the organization that had apparently tried to wipe out the human race.

I halted in mid-step, my heart pounding hard enough to be heard from across the room . . . if anyone had been paying attention.

Brenda was bent over the table, dangerously close to the orb. "How'd you get this?"

The professor folded his arms. "Yesterday I went back to Dr. Mathis's lab at the aquarium. The police were there, of course, and a guy from management was telling them about a case of vandalism. While he was holding their attention, I slipped in and walked directly to the spot where Tank had destroyed one of the orbs."

"Didn't anyone stop you?" Brenda asked.

"Of course not. I had borrowed one of their lab coats." The professor's smile deepened. "If you wear a lab coat and behave as though you know what you're doing, most people will defer to your authority."

"And this orb was just lying on the floor?" I asked, embarrassed to hear a tremor in my voice.

"It was shattered, the pieces resting where Tank left them. I put all the bits and chips into a specimen tray and carried it out. Note that, please. The orb was in at least a dozen pieces. It looked nothing like this."

Despite my innate abhorrence of the object, the professor's comment sparked my curiosity. "A substitution," I suggested. "Someone took the broken orb and left this sphere."

He shook his head. "Once I reached my car, I placed the tray in a box and sealed it. I slept with the box under my bed at the Goldstein's. I didn't break the seal until this morning and *this* is what I found."

My gaze drifted back to the orb, which didn't have a single scratch or blemish.

"I ain't buying the idea that this thing put itself back together," Brenda said. "So maybe someone saw you take it. Maybe there's a GPS in all those pieces, so someone tracked it. A good inside man could have switched it out while you were asleep and you'd never hear a peep."

The professor shook his head. "When I opened the box at the Goldsteins', the orb had regained its spherical shape, but I could see ridges in the metal—or what I *assume* is metal. I put the box in my car and drove here. When I opened the box a few moments ago, it looked exactly as it does now—perfectly smooth."

The atmosphere thickened with the silence of concentration. One by one, we pulled out chairs and sat, our gazes fixed on the orb. And as we watched and thought and theorized, I couldn't help feeling that the orb was staring back at us.

"Any markings at all?" Brenda asked, tapping the orb's silver surface with her fingernail. "I take it you didn't find a spot stamped 'Made in China'?"

"No markings—in this incarnation, at least. And I didn't see any in its first incarnation, either. Then again, I was fighting the thing, so it would have been difficult to give it a thorough examination."

"Are you certain the surface is smooth?" I asked. "There could be a pattern too small to be seen without magnification."

The professor pulled a magnifying glass from his pocket and slid it toward me. "Be my guest."

Brenda tapped the orb and sent it rolling toward me. I put out a hand to catch it, and the instant my fingertips made contact, something began to buzz in my head. I closed my eyes, wondering if my ears were playing tricks on me, but like a radio tuner honing in on the correct frequency, the buzz disappeared and the voices began.

Any god that desires worship is arrogant and vain; you are the source of knowledge.

Faith is useless. Knowledge is all-powerful.

Become enlightened. You are god. Knowledge is the source of all power.

I dropped the magnifying glass and pushed away from the table. The voices were so loud that I could no longer hear my friends. Squinting in annoyance and anxiety, I mumbled something about a headache and stood. I tried to walk back into the living room, but stumbled into the half wall that served as a room divider.

Seek knowledge, and become one of us.

You are not a being, you are becoming.

Belong to us. We are the enlightened, the powerful.

I felt strong hands on my shoulders, then someone turned me around. Tank stood before me, his face filled with concern, his mouth opening and closing, but I couldn't hear a word. All I could hear were the voices and their incessant chatter.

Tank looked away and said something else, then the professor appeared in my field of vision, his brows drawn into knots of worry. He said something to me, then snapped his fingers before my eyes. Why?

Next thing I knew, he had guided me to the couch and pressed on my shoulders, forcing me to sit. Brenda, Tank, the professor, and Daniel stood around or sat on the coffee table and stared at me, their lips moving in time to the voices in my head. Was I hallucinating, too?

Everything you've heard about God is a lie.
There is neither good nor evil; there is only knowledge.
Once you become enlightened, everything becomes clear.
God desires slaves; you deserve freedom.
Freedom is knowledge.
You are god.
You are—
Knowledge is all.
Join us.

Unable to listen a minute more, I closed my eyes and snapped "Shut up!", but the voices only spoke faster and higher, as if someone had increased the speed on an old record player. I clenched my fists, frustrated by my inability to block out the sounds.

God is a lie.
Knowledge—
Freedom—
New music—
Join us!

I threw back my head and screamed, then crumpled into darkness.

Chapter 2

I sat in an office waiting room, arms crossed, hands fisted. Professor McKinney sat at my left to keep me from bolting, and Daniel sat at my right, because I figured if anyone knew psychiatrists, he did. Brenda sat next to Daniel, because where he went, she went, and Tank sat next to Brenda because he didn't want to be left behind. "We're a team," he had reminded me as we left the rental house. "So if all the others are going, I'm goin' too."

I was present under protest, because seeing a shrink was the last thing I wanted to do. But the professor had made a deal—when the medics who responded to his 911 call wanted to take me to the hospital's behavioral unit, the professor talked them out of it by promising that he'd take me to a shrink as soon as possible.

So here we were.

I closed my eyes and let my head tip back to the wall. After I fainted yesterday, I woke to a young guy shining a flashlight into my eyes. "She's awake," he called, while voices behind him murmured. Only when he snapped his light off did I see the professor and company standing behind the medics, all of them wearing expressions of grave concern.

"I'm okay," I told them, sitting up. "It's just that I kept hearing voices—"

That offhand comment nearly landed me back in psych. Mentally healthy people apparently do not walk around hearing voices. People can talk to themselves, their dead aunt, or the dog, but if another voice joins the chorus, extreme steps must be taken.

Later that night, the professor knelt on the edge of the couch and placed a paternal hand on my shoulder. "Andi, it's only natural that you feel some aftereffects from our experience with that nasty fungus. I've felt an odd moment or two myself, and you were, shall we say, under the influence a lot longer than I was."

"You've been touching the orb," I said. "Has touching it ever made you . . . hear anything?"

His brows rushed together. "Never."

That's when I agreed to see a psychiatrist, but after a good night's sleep and a decent breakfast, I no longer felt the need to have my head examined.

"Who is this Dr. Drummond, anyway?" I asked, turning to the professor. "I live in this area, you know. My grandparents will have to deal with any fallout if he decides I'm crazy."

The professor gave me an indulgent smile. "I asked your family doctor for a recommendation when you went in for that emergency check-up. He said Dr. Drummond would be perfect for you—he has a sterling reputation in the international medical community, and he's in the area temporarily, working on some research project as a visiting fellow. He's British. Won't be around long enough to gossip, so you can tell him anything you like."

"Even about our work?"

The professor's smile twisted. "Well . . . you might want to be discreet in that area. Tell him only what you must."

I snorted softly, then looked at the others. "I hope you all know that a person's visits to a psychiatrist are private. I appreciate the group support, but I'm going into that office alone."

"Noted," Brenda said, an unlit cigarette dangling from her lips. "Not that I wanted to go with you, but okay."

I leaned forward. "You know, this shrink might be able to help you lick that smoking habit."

"I'm licking it just fine, thanks," she answered, the tip of her nicotine placebo bobbing with each syllable. "Daniel's helpin' me."

"How?" I asked.

"He put the ButtOut app on my phone. It tracks how much money I'm savin' by not buying cigarettes, how much tar isn't goin' into my lungs, and how many extra days I get to live. I guess that's what you call positive—um, positive—"

"Positive reinforcement."

When I supplied the missing word, McKinney patted my shoulder. "See? Your mind is fine; you're as sharp as ever. I'm sure you were only suffering some kind of hangover from residual . . . you know."

I closed my eyes. Oh, yeah, we were *fine*. We knew about two deaths that hadn't been made public and we'd seen things that would strike fear into the hardest cop on the local force. No wonder I was having trouble clearing my head.

My eyes opened automatically when I heard the click of a door knob. Looking up, I saw casual slip-on shoes, khakis, a short-sleeved knit shirt, and the most gorgeous face I had ever seen on a man—cleft chin, sparkling blue eyes, longish black hair, and a toothpaste-commercial smile. For a moment my mind went completely blank, then I heard him speak: "Andrea Goldstein?"

Brenda elbowed me. "If you want, I could take your place in there."

"I'm okay," I whispered, rising on wobbly knees and following the man into his office.

I don't know what I expected to find in Dr. Drummond's office—a couch, maybe? But all I saw was a desk, a couple of leather wing chairs, and a laptop computer on a wooden stand—a classy version of those rolling bedside tables they used in hospitals.

But before I even moved toward the chairs, Dr. Drummond looked at me, smiled, and held out his hand. "Hamish Drummond," he said in his lilting accent. "It's a pleasure to meet you."

I swallowed hard and shook his hand, taking care to make sure my grip was firm and polite. I didn't know how a shrink might evaluate an introductory handshake, but I wanted him to see that I was a normal young adult, not a hysteric.

Dr. Drummond gestured to a wing chair. I thanked him and sat, then he took the chair near the computer stand. "So," he said, crossing one knee and looking at me with an open, pleasant expression. "What brings you to my office today?"

That voice! The professor had said he was from Britain, but this wasn't a London accent—it was Irish, or perhaps Scottish. One of those lovely speech patterns that made everything sound musical. I contemplated asking where he was from, but didn't want him to think I was changing the subject.

"What do you already know?" I asked. "I don't want to waste your time."

He opened his hands and grinned. "Can you believe it?

I know nothing. So why don't you tell me what you think I ought to know."

"I don't want to keep you here all day."

"I have as long as it takes—almost." A dimple in his cheek winked at me as he smiled. "Tell me the important things; then tell me about the thing that brought you here."

I drew a deep breath, then exhaled in a rush. "My name is Andi Goldstein. I was studying humanities in college when I met professor James McKinney, who's now my employer. I actually grew up in this area, and graduated from Ponce de Leon High school. I guess this is what you'd call my hometown."

He propped his elbow on the chair and rested his chin on his hand. "Don't you enjoy coming home?"

"Sure. I get to see Sabba and Safta, of course, and Abby, my dog. I didn't take her after graduation because I travel a lot and she's getting old. But she is always happy to see me."

On and on I talked. I told him about being a geek in high school. I told him about my gift of seeing patterns everywhere, in numbers, fabrics, and events. I told him I'd been adopted by my grandparents, that they were devout Jews who raised me with a bat mitzvah and everything, and that I still considered myself religious . . . to a point. "I believe in God," I said, "but I don't talk about him much because it's a personal thing. But . . . lately I've begun to wonder about all the things I believed growing up. I've realized that evil exists, and that sometimes it exists just for evil's sake."

Dr. Drummond's brows lowered. "I'm not sure I get your meaning."

"Well," I shrugged, "when you read about a serial killer, you usually learn that he came from an abusive family, or that he never bonded to his mother as a baby, or he was mentally deficient or something. You rarely hear about criminals who are bad because they enjoy hurting others. I didn't believe that was possible until lately, but now I have to wonder."

"What are you wondering?"

I blew out a breath and glanced at the clock. "My goodness! I've been talking for a solid hour. And I haven't even gotten to the stuff about why I'm here."

The doctor checked his watch, then smiled. "Can you give me an abridged version?"

"Sure." I leaned forward. "Those people out in the waiting room—they're friends, and we've been investigating unusual situations. Ever since I joined up with them, we've all seen things I can't explain." Because I felt completely comfortable, I told him about Sridhar and the Institute, about the disappearing house and what the professor called *posthumous manifestations*. I told him about the bird and fish die-offs, about the odd girl that managed to contact us through another universe, and our mad romp through Europe and a half dozen multiverses. Finally, I told him about the green fungi, the flying orbs, and how I almost died.

"The fungus is no longer in my body," I said, "but yesterday I thought I heard the voices again . . . and they were loud enough to drown out everything else. I don't know what's happening, but at times I'm scared spitless. Being out of control—having intruders in my brain—was the most frightening experience of my life. That's what happened yesterday, and I was so frightened that I fainted. That's why I'm here."

I sat perfectly still and waited for Dr. Drummond to slap his head in disbelief or something, but he simply smoothed a wrinkle out of his pant leg and leaned toward me. "Andrea," he asked, his blue eyes darkening with concern, "in this moment, right now, what do you want more than anything else in the world?"

I blinked. "I want to get out of here."

He laughed. "Fair enough. What will you want when you're in the car and on your way home?"

I thought a moment. "I want . . . to feel like myself again. I want to feel bubbly and optimistic and bright . . ." I looked down and laughed. "Sounds like a line from *I Feel Pretty*, doesn't it?"

"Pretty and witty and bright," Dr. Drummond joked, and when I glanced at him, his eyes danced with a conspiratorial gleam.

My heart did a flip flop. He knew *Westside Story*?

"I have a favor to ask," he said, standing and moving behind his desk. He opened a drawer, then pulled out a slender blue notebook, the kind we had used in college for essay tests. "I'm going to give you a blank journal, and I want you to fill three pages in it every day, without fail. Write about what you're thinking and feeling, what you're doing, that sort of thing. Don't worry about spelling or grammar; this isn't for publication. It's just for you."

He thumbed through the blank book as if checking to be sure the pages were clean, then came around the desk and handed it to me. "And I'd like to see you again in a few days. We'll talk some more, and maybe you'll discover that you've written something important in your wee book. If that's so, you can tell me about it. Here's my card. Call me if you have a problem."

I put the card in my pocket, then clutched the blank journal. "My wee book." I smiled at it, clean and compact, waiting for my words. "All right, I'll see you in a couple of days."

Chapter 3

The next morning, the professor received three boxes from a FedEx truck, then dragged all of them into the living room. A UPS truck pulled up five minutes later, and handed over a package addressed to Brenda.

"What's all that?" Brenda asked, looking at the boxes as if they were bombs that might go off at any moment.

The professor closed the door and looked at our suddenly crowded living room. "The large boxes are from a clipping service," he said. "This one is for you, Barnick, from a Mrs. Irene Brown."

"Auntie Rene!" Brenda practically vaulted over the coffee table to reach the professor, then snatched the box.

I stared in shock—Brenda never showed that much enthusiasm—while the professor gave her a disapproving frown. "Have you been sharing our address?"

"Only with Auntie Rene." Brenda lowered her brow. "You got a problem with that?"

"We must think of our personal security. No matter who we're communicating with, email accounts can be hacked, cell phone calls can be recorded—"

"Auntie Rene would never hurt me," Brenda said, tearing into the package. "The woman worries about me every time I go out of town. She's a little over-protective, but still—" Brenda held up what looked like a seriously deformed orange hammer. Instead of a head and a prong, the top of this hammer featured two formidable steel knobs.

Tank gaped at it. "What in the—"

"The Life Hammer," Brenda said, reading from a card. "Dear Brenda—I looked on a map and saw where you is and then I saw that long bridge over the ocean. Cars fall into the water every day, and I don't want you drownin', so I got this for you. Keep it in your purse and if your car falls in, just smack the window.

"I've also enclosed a can of shark repellant, in case you go swimmin' at the beach, and some mosquito wipes. They're not for wiping mosquitoes, they're for keeping them away because they carry that nasty West Nile virus. Don't want you gettin' sick. Love you, Auntie Rene."

I laughed, Tank guffawed, and even Daniel smiled. "Hoo boy," Brenda said, chuckling herself, "when was the last time a car went into the water around here?"

"About the same time somebody got the West Nile virus," the professor said. "Or was attacked by a shark."

I shook my head. "You guys shouldn't laugh about things like that. I don't think any cars have gone over the bridge lately, but about thirty years ago, a bunch of cars and a bus went into the bay. A ship hit the bridge, so it was a pretty big deal."

"That was a long time ago," Brenda said, "but it was nice of Auntie Rene to think about me."

She set the orange hammer, shark repellent, and mosquito wipes on the coffee table, but Daniel picked them up and handed them back to her. "Keep," he said, his eyes serious.

She looked at him, then sighed. "Little man, what am I gonna do with you?" Still she dropped all of her aunt's gifts into her purse. "Better?"

Daniel nodded and went back to playing a game on his new phone.

"Now," the professor said, pulling one of the large boxes over to his chair. "Let's get to work."

"What's a clipping service?" Tank asked.

The professor ripped the tape from his box, then opened it and pulled out a stack of printed pages. "Several times now we've had people mention an organization called the Gate, so I thought we should investigate them. Right after the event at the school I subscribed to a media monitoring service and asked for printed copies of articles that mention the group." He smiled with satisfaction as he lifted out a second stack. "And here they are . . . three boxes filled with clippings."

Brenda groaned. "You expect us to read through all that?"

"Time to change our tactics," the professor said. "Ever since we got together we've been reactive, simply responding to the odd things we encountered. We were being played, rattled, used, and for what? Nothing. We have nothing to show for our efforts."

"We're alive," I pointed out. "That's something."

The professor waved a hand in my direction, but charged ahead. "We are not merely reacting any longer," he said, his voice booming in the small house. "We are going to be proactive. We are going to learn everything we can about this group. We're going to figure out who or what the Gate is, and then we're going to rattle their cage for a while."

He pulled another stack of printed clippings and set it

in front of Tank.

Tank grinned. "You mean we're gonna turn the tables on 'em?"

"Exactly." The professor set another stack in front of Brenda. "Here's the plan. Andi and I will work on the orb while Tank and Brenda skim these clippings. You'll find the pertinent parts highlighted, see? If the information is useful, circle the important sections and set the clipping aside. If the article isn't helpful, toss it into an empty box."

Brenda lifted a stack of pages onto her lap, then scowled at McKinney. "You do know that you could do the same thing with Google, right? For free? And without killing a bunch of trees?"

He shook his head. "I want information that would never find its way to the World Wide Web. I want facts that precede the Internet. Humor me, please, and start reading."

Tank took a stack of documents and went to sit by the window; Brenda stretched out on the couch. Daniel sat on the floor tapping his phone, but his gaze kept darting around the room, leaving me to wonder what he was seeing . . .

"Andi?" The professor went into the dining room and pulled out a chair. Sighing, I joined him.

From a cardboard box, the professor lifted a scale, a drill, and a tape measure. I reached for my tablet computer, then opened a scratch pad.

"You know the routine," McKinney said. "Weigh, measure, record. Experiment. Then let's see what this little odd ball is made of."

The orb, I discovered, weighed four pounds, ten ounces—in the hour I measured it, at least. The circumference was fourteen inches exactly, and when I held it twelve inches from the floor and released it, it fell to the linoleum with a thud. "Definitely not weightless," I typed on my tablet. "Incapable of flight, as far as I can tell."

The professor plugged in the electric drill, which he fitted with the smallest drill bit. He took eye protectors from his bag, which we both put on. Then, beneath that awful chandelier, the professor held the orb between his hands while I attempted to drill into it. I was unsuccessful when I held the drill at a ninety degree angle to the surface, but when I tilted the drill slightly, the bit did leave a thin scratch along the surface.

"Not impermeable, then," the professor said, lifting his protective eyewear to study the scratch. "A laser could make quick work of it."

I smiled. "Got one of those in your box?"

"If only."

We left the orb. I went to the kitchen for a soft drink while the professor stood to stretch.

"I don't get it," Tank called, looking up. "Most of the articles say the Gate doesn't exist. That it's a bogeyman invented to scare people."

"Scare them with what?" the professor asked. "Nuclear war? Disease?"

"Nothing is ever spelled out," Brenda said, "at least not in what I'm reading. People talk about the group, but no personal names are ever mentioned."

"But what if the Gate was hiding in plain sight?" I said. "Wouldn't that be brilliant?"

"Hard to know truth from rumor." Brenda handed a document to Daniel, who dropped it in the "not useful" box. "I mean, some of the articles claim the Gate goes all the way back to medieval times; others say the old Gate is gone and new people have revived the organization."

"Wait a minute." Obeying a hunch, I grabbed my laptop. I booted it, then used my cell phone to create a hot spot. Two minutes later, I was on the Internet. I typed a name, hit enter, and landed on a web page.

"Take a look," I said, turning the computer so Tank and Brenda could see. "The Gate has a web page and a Twitter account."

"Get out!" Brenda came over to read the text at the top of the screen. "Wake up, weary traveler! This war-infested, polluted world is nearly at its end. Join us as we prepare for a new society, an age of personal power and enlightenment. Join those of us who have realized secrets the ancients possessed, secrets for which others have died in order to safeguard the future."

"Gobbledygook," the professor mumbled. "If the secrets are so great, why not employ them now?"

"No names or photos on that site," Tank observed, studying the page. "If this organization is so cool, why won't anyone admit being a part of it?"

"Let me see that." The professor stepped out of the dining room and stood between Tank and Brenda, all of them studying the website. "Hmm. Maybe I should have Googled them."

"According to this site, the cloud of secrecy is about to evaporate." Brenda pointed to a text box in the lower corner and read aloud: "The Gate is a powerful collective of leaders entrusted with protecting the billions of human beings on the planet. Our plan for mankind has spanned several eras and prevented humanity from engaging in acts that would have destroyed all human life. The scale of our operation requires stealth, leaving no overt proof of our work. But the time for covert operations and anonymity is nearing an end."

"Typical end of the world stuff." The professor shook his head. "Fodder for the apocalypse survivalists."

"What are they gonna do?" Tank looked at me, eyes wide. "Don't they realize God wins in the end?"

"Maybe they don't believe in God." Brenda pulled her cigarette from her back pocket, stuck it in her mouth, and squinted at the screen. "Looks like they believe in themselves more than anything else."

"They believe in knowledge." The answer came easily because I'd heard the words in my head only a few days before. "They believe the key to a better life is enlightenment."

Tank laughed. "That's what the devil promised Eve in the garden, you know. She ate from the Tree of Knowledge of Good and Evil, and when she'd finished, she had new knowledge, all right. She'd been living in a perfect and good world, but that forbidden fruit gave her firsthand knowledge of evil and sin. Knowledge isn't everything it's cracked up to be."

"I don't think we can be so simplistic," the professor said, frowning. "There are levels to man's knowledge, and men have always wanted to better themselves, to rise above their beginnings—"

"That's what Satan wanted, too." Tank's jaw jutted forward. "He was a beautiful angel, designed to serve God, but he wanted to rise about his station and be equal with God."

"So you think it's wrong for a guy to be ambitious?" Brenda asked.

"Not necessarily. But it's wrong for a man to be proud. Every time I get to feelin' that I'm more special than somebody else, God lets me know that I'd be nothin' without the gifts and grace he's given me. I'm just a man, the professor's just a man—"

The professor raised a brow. "So my years of education count for nothing?"

I closed my eyes as their words flowed over me. A vein in my temple had begun to throb, so I pressed my fingertips to the spot in a vain attempt to massage the tightness away. I did not want to hear the voices again, and even hearing about the Gate felt like opening a door to the intruders.

"Excuse me." I closed my laptop and stood, then moved toward the hallway that led to the bedrooms. Before leaving, I turned to the others. "I have a headache, so I'm going to lie down where it's quiet."

At any other time, the professor would have made a crack about my inexhaustible energy, but my comment left him—left all of them—speechless. They didn't want a repeat performance with EMTs and flashing lights, either.

They looked at me, their eyes shining with concern, and then they let me go.

I rode aboard a dream ship that pulled up to a dock and regurgitated passengers onto shore. I walked across the sand and into a large room that seemed to be some sort of auditorium. I could see silhouetted heads and shoulders, and hear sibilant whispers in the darkness.

I lifted my gaze and saw a lighted stage at the far end of the room. A woman in a flowing white tunic stood on the stage, and she lifted a woven basket and set it on a tree stump. Then I heard the sound of a baby's cry. The crowd buzzed, but since no one seemed inclined to intercede for the child, I moved down the aisle, my gaze fixed on the basket.

Three steps led up to the stage. I mounted them slowly, wondering if someone would come rushing out from backstage to apprehend me for trespassing. The woman watched me, her eyes like large liquid pools, but she did nothing to impede my progress.

Finally I reached the basket, where the baby's cries had softened to a soft mewling.

A gauzy fabric covered the opening, so I pulled it away and gazed on a baby with a misshaped head. Or not exactly misshaped—the head was *fluid*, the skull moving beneath the skin, rearranging the mouth, nose, and eyes, of which there were three. The eyes positioned themselves into a straight line, then the lips smacked while the eyes shifted again, one eye moving to the center of the forehead. The infantile mouth curled in a smile, and the eyes—now blue—slowly blinked at me.

The baby was *me*. I knew it as surely as I knew my name.

I staggered backward, my body caught in a paralysis of

horror. The woman looked at me and smiled. "She is not settled yet. Her father alone has the right to say what she will become."

At the mention of the child's father, I sensed a presence and heard the deep, rattling breath of a dark creature. Compelled to turn, I looked for the source of the sound and saw horns, yellow eyes with dark slashes for pupils, and brilliant, tiger teeth . . . and then I screamed.

I woke and clutched at my blanket, then listened to the soft sounds of Brenda's breathing until my heart rate decreased and my palms stopped perspiring. Then I closed my eyes and prayed that I would not dream again.

Chapter 4

After a restless night, I found Tank and Daniel at the kitchen bar the next morning, both of them slurping down bowls of Lucky Charms and focused on their phones.

"Take that," Tank said, dropping his spoon so he could work the phone with both hands. "You're sunk, kid!"

"Morning," I mumbled, then I moved to the fridge and took out a bottle of orange juice.

I grimaced as a shrill, undulating siren pierced the quiet of the kitchen and I nearly dropped the orange juice when a robotic voice called MEGADEATH APPROACHING, CAPTAIN. DEFEND YOUR BATTLESHIP.

While Tank grinned, Daniel's fingers flew over his phone. "What are you guys *doing*?" I shouted, holding my free hand over my ears as horns and sirens continued to wail.

"Saved!" Daniel grinned at Tank as the kitchen went silent again.

Tank looked up at me. "It's *Battleship Megadeath*," he said. "Daniel's really into the game. He's playing eighty-seven other players right now—some of them in other countries."

"I hope the other players don't wake up their mates," I said, jerking my thumb toward the bedrooms where Brenda and the professor still slept. "I've never heard anything like that."

"The siren only goes off if your battleship is sinking. Oh . . . gotta take care of this . . . there." Tank grinned again, then swept up a spoonful of Lucky Charms. "It's addictive. If your ship is hit, the siren goes off until you either save your ship or it goes under."

"For my sake, then, I hope neither of you loses any ships. My ears can't take it."

"Play," Daniel said, looking at me.

"Daniel, I don't know—"

"You'll find an invite in your email," Tank said. He tilted his head toward Daniel. "Come on, humor the kid. You might enjoy it."

"Maybe."

I went to the pantry next, and stared at the shelves—a cereal variety pack, a box of cheese crackers, two bags of potato chips, four boxes of brown sugar cinnamon Pop Tarts, and a canister of beef jerky. Clearly, one of the men had done the grocery shopping.

I pulled a package of pop tarts from the box, then ripped it open and took a bite. One stool remained vacant at the kitchen bar, but as I walked toward it, the dining room table caught my eye. The orb was still in the center, but someone had covered it with a dishtowel.

I lowered my pop tarts and peered at the towel. "What's up with this?" I asked the guys. "Who covered it?"

"Guilty." Tank raised his hand. "Did it last night. Daniel kept sayin' that the thing was watchin' him."

"Really, Daniel?" I leaned on the counter to look him in the eye. "Do you know that for certain, or did it just feel like they were watching you?"

Daniel looked up from his phone, met my gaze . . . and shrugged.

Sighing, I walked to the table, then pulled the dishtowel away from the orb. Nothing happened, but the orb looked different. Yesterday it had been a shiny silver color; now it was gold. Why hadn't I thought to record its color when I was making notes?

"Hey guys." I gestured to the orb when they turned around. "Notice anything different?"

Tank nodded. "It's gold."

Daniel nodded, too. "Bigger."

I lifted a brow, then reached for the professor's bag. A quick wrap with the tape measure proved Daniel's point: the orb was now fourteen and one-half inches, so the thing had expanded . . . unless I measured incorrectly yesterday.

I picked up the orb and turned it in my hand, searching for the scratch. I spun it from east to west, then from north to south, but the scratch had disappeared.

I sank to one of the dining room tables and propped my chin in my hand. Unless my eyes were deceiving me, the orb had healed itself. And if Daniel was correct—and he often was—the thing had some kind of consciousness. It was aware of us.

Dear Journal:

Living things share seven characteristics—let's see if I can remember all of them:

- Living things are composed of cells.

- Living things have different levels of organization.
- Living things use energy.
- Living things respond to their environment.
- Living things grow.
- Living things reproduce.
- Living things adapt to their environment.

Of those seven characteristics, so far I have seen the orb expand (and contract), respond to its environment (perhaps), and appear to heal itself . . . which must have used energy.

So is this thing alive?

"Whacha doin'?" Brenda asked, glancing at my journal. "You workin' already?"

"Just making notes." I jerked my head toward the orb. "Notice anything different?"

Brenda glanced at it, then her eyes widened. "Have we struck gold?"

"It's not actual gold," I said, "but it did change color."

"Why?"

"I've no idea."

We both looked toward the front door when the professor came in—apparently he'd been up and out long before us. He strode into the dining room and dropped the morning paper on the table.

I glanced at the front page headline, then looked at him. "Something special in there?"

"Couple of things," the professor said, crossing his arms. "First, the police are investigating the disappearance of Dr. Tom Mathis and Nick Warner. Neither man has been seen in days, but they found a trace of Mathis's DNA at Ponce de Leon High School. So they've tied the damage at his lab to the mess at the school, and now they're saying he met with foul play."

Brenda and I looked at each other. We were all pretty sure about what had happened to Nick Warner, but we certainly weren't going to call the paper with news about the killer fungus that may or may not have been created by the Gate and/or cooperative aliens. As for Tom Mathis, we'd been with him when his body exploded into a cloud of green powder. No way we were sharing *that* news with anyone.

"Do you—" I caught the professor's gaze, "—think we should go to the police? If they're looking for bodies, they're not going to find anything."

"I don't know." He scratched his chin. "I doubt they'd believe us."

"If my dog was carrying that killer fungus, I'd want to know," Tank said, turning to join in the conversation. "If they've unleashed another batch of that stuff, people could be dying right now."

"I don't think they will release it any time soon," the professor said. "Call it a hunch, but I think they were simply testing that fungus. After the birds and fish, Nick Warner, Andi, and Dr. Mathis stepped into the role of human guinea pigs, so the researchers now have verified results of their experiment." He shook his head. "If they launch that fungus again, I believe it'll be on a global scale. Not much sense in tipping your hand before your first major attack."

I folded the newspaper, about to draw the professor's attention to the orb, but he took the paper from me. "Don't throw this away," he said. "Mathis is having a memorial service today. Maybe we should go."

Brenda lifted her head. "I don't do funerals, especially for people I barely knew."

"A memorial service isn't the same thing," I pointed out. "There's no body."

"I'll go," Tank said. "Mathis was a nice man before the fungus got a hold of him. I think we should all go."

The professor smiled. "Mathis's likability is a moot point. Statistics indicate that killers often visit the funerals or graves of their victims just to revel in the experience. I don't know if we'll see members of the Gate at that memorial service, but surely time spent honoring a fellow scientist is time well-spent."

"Whatever," Tank said, grinning at me. "What time do we leave?"

"Eleven." The professor glanced at his watch. "Which gives all of you just enough time to get ready."

I took three steps toward the bedroom I was sharing with Brenda, but even though I'd been forewarned, I wasn't ready for what came next: MEGADEATH APPROACHING, CAPTAIN. DEFEND YOUR BATTLESHIP.

As horns and sirens blared from Daniel's phone, I looked at Brenda, who had spilled her coffee and looked as though someone had nearly run her over. "Come on," I said, raising my voice to be heard above the noise. "I'll explain everything while we're getting ready."

Dear Journal:

Thomas Mathis, as it turned out, was neither religious nor prepared for death, so the funeral director is holding Mathis's memorial service in the cemetery where his daughter insisted on purchasing a plot.

I overheard all the pertinent details while washing my hands in the ladies' room. "I kept telling that man that I wanted a place where I could sit and grieve for Daddy," a voice called from the first of the two stalls. "He said, 'But we don't have a body!' and I said, 'Well, pretend we do!' It's bad enough that we don't know why Daddy's DNA was all over that school, but I won't have people thinking I was too cheap to buy my dad a proper headstone."

I glanced at the red-faced older woman who stood by the paper towels, then gave her a sympathetic smile. Poor thing—I hope she wasn't Dr. Mathis's mother.

I left the restroom and followed a series of discreet signs to an open plot surrounded by about two dozen people. A fiberboard casket sat on some kind of mechanism, and a spray of roses—probably from the distraught daughter—lay on the coffin.

I found myself wishing I could step up and tell the mourners the truth about the marine biologist's fate:

Excuse me, ladies and gentlemen—most of you are wondering what happened to Dr. Mathis, and I hope you'll be pleased to know he is no longer suffering. His mind was abducted by some sort of collective consciousness and his body was taken over by a green fungus that eventually caused him to explode at the high school. He is now at rest and his soul is wherever souls go under these circumstances, so maybe we should give the roses to someone who needs them and put the casket back in storage.

The touch of a hand on my shoulder startled me and I nearly jumped out of my skin.

"Whoa." Coming alongside me, Brenda gave me a quizzical look. "You okay? You're not usually wired this tight."

"I'm fine." I stuck my journal in my purse, then crossed my arms. "You?"

"I was going to ask you somethin', but I don't want to put ideas in your head."

"Okay. What did you want to ask?"

"Just look around," Brenda said, her gaze drifting over the crowd. "As the dude talks, tell me if you see anyone who looks familiar."

I scanned the people at the graveside. "Do I know this person?"

"Not gonna say anything else. Just take your time and tell me if you spot anyone we've seen before."

I sighed, then transferred my gaze to the funeral director as he moved to the head of the casket. He welcomed the guests, then read Mathis's newspaper obituary. As he rambled on, I studied the guests—Mathis's daughter stood next to the open grave, supported by a group of older women. A few middle-aged couples stood behind them. No children anywhere, as far as I could see, but it was a school day. A group of twenty-somethings stood in a knot behind the funeral director, and I recognized some of them from the aquarium where Mathis had worked. Were they the familiar faces Brenda was referring to? Shifting my gaze, I saw a handful of other adults, probably friends or neighbors, and Sridhar—

I blinked. Between two bald men I saw a guy who looked like Sridhar Rajput, the young man we had met at the Institute for Advanced Psychic Studies, one of many enterprises reportedly sponsored and/or managed by the Gate. Sridhar had been one of the Institute's star pupils, specializing in lucid dreaming and dream telepathy. He had wanted out of the program so we tried to help him escape, but he vanished from Brenda's apartment in the middle of the night.

What was he doing *here?*

I turned to Brenda and caught her eye, then mouthed the name: *Sridhar?*

Her eyes widened, then she smiled and nodded.

I turned to make contact with our friend, but I could

no longer see him. Was he trying to make his way to us?

"And now," the funeral director said, "let us observe a moment of silent meditation in honor of the deceased."

I lowered my head and closed my eyes, not willing to see any other oddities in the crowd. Silence wrapped around us, a heavy quiet marred only by the quiet swishing of cars moving on the road several yards away. A bird warbled in one of the wide oak trees, and the wind gently ruffled a ribbon dangling from the roses on the casket.

Then the sound of horns and sirens blasted the gathering. MEGADEATH APPROACHING, CAPTAIN. DEFEND YOUR BATTLESHIP.

As the sirens wailed and horns blared, Tank, Brenda, and I fumbled for our phones. Brenda dumped her purse, then knelt to sort through all the things that had fallen into the grass. Tank pulled his phone from his pocket and was frantically punching buttons; I took my phone from the special pocket inside my purse and slid my finger over the screen again and again, vainly searching for the *Battleship Megadeath* icon. I had accepted Daniel's invitation and downloaded the game right before leaving the house, and though I didn't even know I *had* a battleship, apparently it was in danger—

From the corner of my eye, I saw the professor pull his phone from his jacket pocket, then tap the screen a few times. The sirens stilled, and the professor folded his hands, his gaze intent on the funeral director.

The noise hadn't come from my phone—or Tank's, or Brenda's. The professor—*really?*—had been the one with the endangered battleship.

My knees went weak as adrenaline stopped spurting through my bloodstream. Kneeling in the grass with a package of cigarettes, her bright orange Life Hammer, can of shark spray, and about a dozen scattered mosquito towelettes, Brenda had begun to mutter under her breath, but I knew she wouldn't say anything to Daniel. We should have muted our phones, and none of us did. Not even the professor.

The funeral director, who had stopped during the initial alarm, resumed his speech. When he finally folded his hands and thanked us for coming, I slipped past Brenda and threaded my way through the dispersing crowd. I kept my head down, not wanting to make eye contact with mourners who might be peeved about the interruption, and ran headlong into a chest that did not yield to my charging advance.

I looked up, my jaw dropping as I stared into the baby blues that had entranced me at our last meeting. "Dr.—Dr. Drummond! What are you doing here?"

He smiled, then squinted as if trying to remember my name. "It's Annie, no, Angie, no—"

"Andi," I told him, feeling a little light-headed. "Andrea Goldstein."

"That's right." He grinned, then stepped aside. "I believe you were intent on leaving."

I managed a weak laugh. "Not really. I thought I saw someone I'd met before."

"Ah. Well. Don't let me keep you."

"It's okay. I don't think he's here . . . more likely I was seeing things. That wouldn't surprise me, especially these days. I've, uh, been a little shaky."

I closed my eyes as a sudden thought occurred. Maybe Brenda hadn't been referring to Sridhar when she mentioned seeing someone we knew. When I mouthed *Sridhar*, she might have thought I was saying *Drummond*. Both names had two syllables.

Dr. Drummond slipped his hands into his pockets. "Been writing in your journal?"

I nodded, glad that I was doing something right. "Every day. Three pages."

"You said you were feeling shaky. Would you like to come in later today? Maybe tomorrow? If you aren't doing well, you don't have to wait until your next appointment."

"But it's Sunday!"

"Aren't all days pretty much alike any more? At least for me they are. Anyway—if you want to come in, please do. You'd be a welcome break from my research work."

I tilted my head, thinking, then nodded. "I think I would like that. Let me check with the professor. If I can get away, I'll give your office a call."

"There is no office—there's only me." He took a business card from his jacket pocket and handed it to me. "When you're a visiting fellow, you don't get to bring along your office staff."

"I understand." I was about to say goodbye and walk away, but I halted when I heard familiar voices. I glanced over my shoulder and saw my team approaching—and every one of them was staring at Dr. Drummond with undisguised curiosity.

The professor was the first to speak. "We saw you the other day," he said, extending his hand, "but we weren't properly introduced. I'm Dr. James McKinney, Andi's employer, and these are our associates—Brenda Barnick, Bjorn Christiansen, and Daniel Patrovski."

Dr. Drummond's brows rose. "You are a unique group."

"You might say that." The professor smiled, but I saw no humor in his eyes.

"Well, we'd better be going. I'll call if I can come in."

I tugged on the professor's arm, but he didn't budge. "I hope you realize," he said, his gaze never leaving Drummond's face, "how special Andi is. She has unique gifts and we rely on her. We expect you to take extremely good care of our girl."

Dr. Drummond eased his hands back into his pockets and smiled. "Och, Andi, I think I've been warned. And dinna you worry, I'll take care of her. I was just tellin' Andi that she ought to come in today for another talk."

The professor looked at me with a shade of rebuke in his eyes. "You didn't say anything about having trouble."

"I'm not, I mean, it's not trouble. It's just . . . I still

don't feel like myself. I keep having odd dreams—"

From out of nowhere, Tank's thick arm wrapped around my shoulder and clamped me to his side. "We'll take good care of her," he told Drummond, smiling broadly. "Because that's what friends do."

"Good to hear." Dr. Drummond smiled again, then looked at me. "I'll be talkin' to you soon, lass."

My cheeks flamed as he walked away. "Good grief," I said, looking from the professor to Tank. "That was a bit much, don't you think?"

"We don't know him," the professor said. "But I like him. He's educated. Cultured. Plus, the man has more degrees than a thermometer."

"I like him, too," Tank said. "Only because he promised to take good care of you."

I looked at Brenda, hoping for a little saltiness to counteract the sweetness, and she didn't disappoint. "Enjoy it while you can," she said, taking Daniel's hand. "It's not every day that you get to be the princess."

Chapter 5

Getting away that afternoon wasn't easy. After we returned from the memorial service, the professor wanted Brenda and Tank to dive back into their reading and he wanted me to conduct experiments with the orb. But I told him I'd do a better job if I could get my head on straight, and Dr. Drummond might be the key to helping me feel like my old self.

Reluctantly, the professor agreed.

So I drove to the building where Dr. Drummond had taken an office. The door was locked, of course, but I knocked and only had to wait a couple of minutes before Drummond let me in. "Sorry about the mess," he said, pointing to a slurry of papers spread over what should have been a receptionist's desk. "And come on back. I'm trying to get my paper ready for a professional publication, and it's kept me so busy I don't have time to tidy up."

I stopped in the hallway. "Are you sure I'm not interrupting? I could back another time."

He smiled. "As I said before, you're a welcome distraction. All work and no diversion makes a psychiatrist a little crazy."

I laughed and dropped into the same wing chair I'd chosen last time. "Did you make that up?"

"That bad, eh?" Drummond dropped into the chair across from me, then casually leaned over the arm. "All right, lass—what's up with you?"

I rubbed my damp palm over my jeans. "I'm having weird dreams." I forced another laugh. "I bet you get that all the time, huh?"

"I hear it a lot, aye. Sometimes our dreams are the way our subconscious speaks to us. But dreams have a unique language."

"Then I definitely don't speak dream."

I watched as Drummond got up and moved to a counter on the other side of the room. The counter held a small sink, a single-serve coffee maker, and a spinner that held about a dozen single serve coffee cups.

"What can I get you?" he asked, turning. "I've got all kinds of coffee, various teas, plus hot cocoa and apple cider."

Considering the steamy weather outside, I wasn't exactly in the mood for a hot drink, but the man was from the United Kingdom. Maybe he preferred teas and coffees out of habit. "Um . . . tea," I said. "Any kind."

"Sugar or the fake stuff?"

"Sugar, please. And cream if you have it."

"I like a woman who knows the proper way to drink tea—though my friends on the other side of the pond would be aghast if they saw me brewing tea with this machine." I heard the hum of the coffee maker, followed by the sound of dribbling liquid. While Drummond prepared the tea, I looked around the office.

The room was more library than office, with tall shelves lining three walls, most loaded with books. Papers and books cluttered the desk in front of a wide window that opened to the parking lot. His laptop sat on the rolling table beside his wing chair, so perhaps he preferred to work away from his desk.

Unlike most doctors, he hadn't hung any degrees or award certificates on the wall, but this was a borrowed space, after all. "No degrees?" I said, glancing back at him.

"Pardon?"

"On the wall—most doctors prominently display their degrees to impress patients."

"Ah." He lifted a steaming mug and brought it over. "University of Edinburgh," he said. "Masters in Psychological Research 2007, Doctorate in Psychology of Individual Differences with an emphasis on Depression and Personality, 2010." He handed me the mug. "I'll hang a few diplomas if you think it will enhance my credibility."

"No need." I felt a blush creep across my cheeks. Did he think I didn't trust him? "So what made you choose psychiatry?"

He chuckled as he sank into his chair. "Fascination, I suppose. People are amazing, and I am easily intrigued. We have so many differences and so many commonalities."

"Sure—some of us are crazy and some aren't."

"I don't think you're crazy, Andrea. You seem completely sane."

"You may not think so after you hear what I've been dreaming."

"If you're ready to tell me, I'd love to listen."

I took a sip of tea, then wiped my hands on my jeans again.

"You're tense," Drummond said. "Why don't you close your eyes and pretend I'm not even in the room?"

I didn't like the idea of closing my eyes—what girl would, with a gorgeous man sitting across from her?—but

ANGELA HUNT

maybe he had a point.

"I've had this dream before," I said, obediently closing my eyes. "I'm in the back of an auditorium, watching a scene. It's dark and there are people all around, but they're only silhouettes. There's a platform down front, and it's lit with bright light. I see a short pedestal with a basket on it, and a blanket is covering whatever's in the basket. A young woman steps out—she's wearing this sort of Grecian gown, all draped and flowing—and she pulls the blanket away. Then I come down the aisle and look into the basket, and somehow I know I'm looking at an infant version of myself. I'm a baby, but I'm not solid—it's like I'm made of flesh without bones, and some invisible force is shaping me. I look at the face—it has three eyes, one in the center of the forehead, then the face shifts so there are only two eyes, but they're horizontal instead of vertical.

"Then the woman says that the child's father has the right to say what the baby will become, and this is what he's chosen, and then I turn and look at a shadowed figure over to the left— it's huge, with horns and wings and scaly skin . . . and I know it's Satan. And the people in the room are chanting things like *you are god* while I'm screaming and the baby's face continues to shift . . . and that's usually when I wake up."

I opened my eyes. Dr. Drummond sat with his elbow propped on the armrest and a finger pressed to his mouth. "Well," he said, smiling across the distance between us, "I can tell you a few basic things about dreams and their meaning. To dream of yourself as an infant means that you want to be nurtured and cared for . . . that you might be feeling a bit unloved. The third eye is supposed to be a window into the spiritual world, so perhaps you've been seein'—or you *want* to see—into other realities. And if you see Satan in your dream—that's a sign of some wrongdoing or evil in your environment." He lifted a brow. "Have I provided any keys that might help you interpret this dream yourself?"

38

"Well . . ." I raked my hand through my hair in the hope that it might stimulate my brain. "Ever since I've become involved with the team, I *have* felt like we're chasing something . . . really evil. In fact, Safta, my grandmother, jokes I've been hanging out with ghostbusters. I tried to tell her that our work is nothing like that, but then again—" I shrugged—"we *have* seen dead people, so maybe she has a point."

"These . . . ghostbusters." Drummond smiled. "Are they the people I met at the funeral?"

"Yes." I tilted my head as a sudden thought struck. "By the way, what were you doing at Dr. Mathis's service?"

"He was the friend of a friend—didn't know him well, but I respected his work."

"His work with jellyfish?"

Drummond's brows lifted, then he smiled and cocked his index finger at me. "He worked primarily with dolphins and manatees, but nice try. Testing my veracity, are you?"

Again, my cheeks burned. "Sorry. But we *have* been chasing evil—and I'm no longer sure who I can trust."

"Back to your dream." Drummond crossed his legs. "You said a blanket covered the baby, and a Grecian goddess-type removed the blanket."

I nodded.

"Could the woman represent your mother? How long has it been since you've seen her?"

My mouth went dry. "My mother," I said, struggling to speak, "was a drug addict. She gave birth to me, then both of us went through detox. But about a month later, someone broke into her apartment and shot her up with enough heroin to kill an elephant, or so the medical examiner said. The police never found the murderer, but they suspected a couple of drug dealers who might have been upset about her leaving that lifestyle behind. The cops turned me over to social services, but my grandparents picked me up before I entered foster care. They adopted me, and I've been living in their home ever since I can remember."

Dr. Drummond listened with his eyes closed, and I watched emotions—sympathy, anger, resignation—flicker over his face as I told the story. When I finished, he grunted softly and looked at me. "Incredible," he said simply, his eyes sparking with interest. "Did your mother use drugs while pregnant with you?"

"Yes. I don't know what she took, but I do know that we were both in the hospital for a while. I'm okay, though. No long term impairment—the doctors say I'm lucky."

"Indeed you are." He shook his head slightly and looked at the chair's armrest. "I suspected that your background might hold some sort of mother/daughter separation because of the woman's role in the dream. She was the *presenter*, you see, just as your mother presented you to the world." A frown line crept between his brows. "Do you know anything about your father?"

"Only that I hope he isn't the devil." I forced a laugh, but the effort sounded weak even to my ears.

"If your birth mother was a heavy drug user, she may not have known who your father was." He hesitated. "The older gentleman with your group—your employer?"

"James McKinney," I said. "And yes, he is a sort of surrogate father figure. I met him in my freshman year, and started working for him right after college graduation. He might appear to be curmudgeonly, but he has a soft heart. It's just buried under layers of logic and rationalization."

"Any sort of romantic—?"

"No," I snapped, having heard the question one time too many. "It is completely possible for an older man and a younger woman to be platonic friends."

"Indeed it is." The doctor looked down, the suggestion of a smile hovering around the corners of his mouth. "Thank you for the background," he said, "now let's talk about the issue that brought you here. Your family doctor said that you experienced a physical trauma and a break from your sense of self. How are you doing physically? And are you beginning to feel more normal?"

"Yes . . . and no."

"Explain, please."

I pressed my lips together and struggled to find the right words. "Yes, I feel strong and I've been getting back to work. But no, because I'm not sleeping much, because I keep having that dream. And sometimes I hear the voices in my head again, but at least this time I'm in control, not them. But shouldn't they be gone? I worry that I'll let my guard down somehow and they'll take over again."

Dr. Drummond leaned forward. "Who are *they*?"

"I don't know. We've heard rumors about a group called the Gate, but we don't know how they are connected to the various situations we've investigated. We're trying to learn all we can, but it's not easy to investigate a group that doesn't want to be investigated."

Dr. Drummond's face cracked into a smile. "Surely you're not serious."

"Why wouldn't I be?"

He shrugged. "The Gate is a favorite topic of conversation among those who like to talk about the Illuminati, the second shooter on the grassy knoll, and the captive aliens at Area 51. No proof exists for any of those things, but the rumors persist."

I stared at the floor. If he didn't believe in the Gate, he wouldn't believe any of my stories.

"Andrea, you're a bright young woman. You don't really believe in the existence of the Gate, do you? You might as well believe in Santa Claus."

"For your information," I said slowly, "Saint Nicholas was an actual man who lived in fourth-century Turkey. Stories of his miracles evolved into the fat man who comes down the chimney on Christmas Eve, but no one can deny that Saint Nicholas existed. Rumors about the Gate and the Illuminati and the second shooter and the aliens may abound, but rumors have to spring from *something*."

"Indeed—fable. Fantasy. As a Scotsman, I can tell you about haunted lochs, fairy hills, and clootie wells. They are part of my heritage, but not part of my reality."

I didn't know what to say. If I told him about some of the things I'd seen . . .

Dr. Drummond drew a deep breath, then settled back in his chair. "I believe that the voices you heard are nothing more than your own anxieties—your subconscious is literally giving voice to your fears. In the same way, your dream is your subconscious way sorting through things your conscious mind puzzled over during the day."

I frowned. "That sounds so simple."

"Most problems usually are." He smiled again. "All right. Let's meet again in a couple of days, but I want you to think about something. I want you to consider hypnotism. It may help you clear out some of your subconscious anxieties. You'll feel better and sleep better, too."

I blinked as my thoughts veered toward nightclub acts and cheesy camp skits. "You want to hypnotize me?"

"I believe you may have memories buried deep in your subconscious, and you'll be more willing to talk about them under hypnosis. It's my job to convince your subconscious self that it's safe for you to put those memories and feelings into words."

I frowned at him. Aside from my recurrent nightmare I couldn't think of any memory horrific enough to be suppressed, but maybe I'd suppressed something I couldn't consciously remember.

"Hypnosis will help you," Drummond said as he opened his laptop, "so I'll pencil you in for Tuesday, if that's all right. We'll have you feeling like yourself in no time."

"I'm still not sure."

"Don't worry, Andi, just think about it. And if you're willing to be hypnotized, we'll have a session when you come in."

I nodded numbly and walked toward the door, more confused than when I'd arrived.

Sunday night, after dining from a half dozen boxes of Chinese food, we gathered in the living room to report on what we'd learned. "First," the professor said, "we'll hear from Daniel." He turned his attention to the boy, who actually looked up from his current game of *Battleship Megadeath*. "Daniel, have you seen anything odd since we've been in Florida? Any—whatever it is you see—that we should be aware of?"

Daniel narrowed his eyes as if thinking, then shook his head.

"Have you seen any of your invisible friends around us since we've been together on this trip?"

Daniel's face brightened.

"Really? Around whom?"

Without hesitation, Daniel pointed to Tank, who grinned an *aw, shucks* grin before replying. "Good to know, Daniel."

The professor lifted his gave to the ceiling as if appealing for help, then continued. "What about Dr. Drummond?" he pressed. "Anything odd about him?"

"No," Daniel said. "No duch. No anioł."

When the professor looked to Brenda for an explanation, she blew out a breath. "Daniel has his own words, and I'm still learnin' some of 'em. But these two I know. From what I can tell, a *duch* is bad. An *anioł* is good."

"So . . .?"

"So Dr. Drummond is not good, not bad."

"Could Daniel come up with something more useful?"

Brenda's brows rushed together. "You wanna back off? He's a *kid*."

"As were we all, once." The professor folded his arms.

"What about your research, Barnick? Have you been able to identify any members of the Gate? Any location? Mission statement? Anything besides what we've already seen on their website?"

"Whaddya think I am, a computer?" Brenda grimaced and pulled some notecards from her oversized purse. "I couldn't find anything linking the Gate to the fungus, but I did find some interesting stuff about funguses."

"That's fungi," the professor corrected. "One fungus, two fungi."

"Whatever. Scientists used to think that fungi evolved from algae because they're both green. But now they think that fungi are more closely related to animals. Fungi don't make food through the sun like plants do; the stuff has a digestive system more like a human's. I don't get all the mumbo-jumbo about why that is—has to do with cells and a bunch of words I can't even pronounce—but I think it might explain why the Gate wanted to use a fungus to do their dirty work."

From the way the professor's eyes widened, I knew he was pleasantly surprised by Brenda's insight. "That *is* interesting, Barnick. What about you, Tank? Any progress?"

"Not really," Tank said, his voice flat. "They do a good job of hiding. Remember when we met Sridhar at the Institute? We also met the director, Dr. Trenton, and Sridhar had heard Trenton acknowledge the school's association with the Gate. But you won't find that published anywhere. Last week, Mathis was babbling about the Gate when the professor and I found him in his lab, but he was infected with the fungus by then, so it wasn't him talking, it was the . . . whatever you want to call it."

"The collective," the professor said. "A hive mentality. When many beings are controlled by a single consciousness."

"Yeah," Tank said. "I know it sounds crazy, but it makes sense once you've seen it in action. So I'm sorry I don't have more to tell you. I found lots of stuff about the Gate, but I can't tell if it's legit or just a bunch of speculation. Clearly, nobody wants to admit they belong to that outfit. Makes it easier to deny that the group even exists."

"Which is also what I discovered." I smiled at Tank, not wanting him to feel discouraged. "By the way, I thought I saw Sridhar at the funeral. Did anyone else see him, or were my eyes playing tricks on me?"

When no one answered, I sighed and moved on. "Chalk it up to my overactive imagination, I guess. Anyway, lots of people on blogs and conspiracy sites blame the Gate for everything from inflation to tsunamis, but no one can prove anything. So yes, the Gate is surrounded by mystery. But on the other hand, they have a website, a Twitter account, and a Pinterest page. All their social media accounts are group accounts, so it's hard to know who's actually posting tweets and blogs, and after a while the posts all sound the same—don't be a slave to a god of any kind; be master of your own life through knowledge, which brings power. Illumination and personal deification—that's pretty much the heart of their message."

"So they're a scapegoat," the professor said, "for everything that goes wrong in the world?"

I shook my head. "They don't take credit for the bad things—they'd probably say that we bring disasters on ourselves. But they always take credit for the good things."

"Like what?" Brenda asked.

"Like the fact that though we have nuclear and hydrogen bombs, we've managed to avoid blowing up the planet," I said. "They'd take credit for nations that sign peace accords. And humans who create art and music."

Tank snorted. "Do they never realize that God is the ultimate artist? That he created a beautiful world? That his angels sang for joy when the earth was formed outta mud? That everything good comes from the creator of all, and we are only reflections of him?"

"Whoa, Cowboy," Brenda said. "Get outta the pulpit. We're trying to stay steady here."

Tank opened his mouth to say something else, then clapped it shut, but I could practically see steam coming out his ears.

"This is good information," the professor said. "Tomorrow I'd like us to focus on the orb. Andi has been studying it, so maybe she'll be ready to give us a report tomorrow."

I lowered my gaze, a little embarrassed that I hadn't been able to finish my work—I'd spent too much time with Dr. Drummond. I didn't want to be the weak link.

"Andi," the professor said, drawing everyone's attention to my flaming face, "are you able to handle all this?"

"Of course." I knew he was speaking out of concern, but I didn't like the extra attention. "I'll make a full report tomorrow."

The professor looked at me for a long moment, then nodded. "Fine," he said. "Just get better."

Chapter 6

I didn't mean to fall asleep in my clothes, but after filling the required three pages in my notebook for Dr. Drummond, I lowered my head to the pillow and closed my eyes. When I awoke, bright sunlight streamed through the window and Brenda was snoring softly in the twin bed across the room.

I must have been exhausted, because impromptu sleeping was foreign to my nature.

I changed out of my rumpled clothes, dashed into the bathroom and dragged a mascara brush across my lashes, then attempted to brush my hair. I glanced in the mirror and saw a pale woman with frizzy red hair staring back at me—the Tim Burton version of Raggedy Ann. But I couldn't help what I looked like, and it wasn't like we were planning to go anywhere.

By the time I made it to the kitchen, the professor had put on the coffee and brought in a huge box of doughnuts. "Wow," I said, lifting the lid. "Guess we're not counting calories this week."

He was standing by the table with a document in his hand, and he waited to finish reading before he looked up and greeted me with a nod. "You could use a few extra calories," he said. "And we're really getting nowhere with all these clippings, right?"

"I think—" I plucked a glazed doughnut from the box, then grabbed a napkin "—we're focusing too narrowly. Instead of spending all day reading about the Gate, maybe one of us should be searching for information on research with fungi, and someone else looking into mechanical orbs."

"Mornin'." Brenda shuffled into the kitchen in her pajamas and slippers, then grabbed her purse from the kitchen counter. "Going outside. If you solve the mysteries of the world, let me know."

I waited until the front door clicked behind her. "You've gotta give her credit," I told the professor. "She's trying hard."

He nodded. "Frankly, I'm surprised she's done as well as she has. What is she down to now, two or three cigarettes a day?"

"Two, I think. She goes out first thing every morning, and right after dinner every night. She only smokes during the day if she's unusually stressed . . . which I guess we've all been these last few days."

The professor didn't argue, but he did look up when Tank lumbered into the kitchen, his outstretched arms punctuating his expressive yawn. "Man," he said, dropping his arms as he shook himself awake. "I slept like a rock. Daniel, too—the kid's still in there sawing logs."

For some reason, my inner alarms clanged. "You sure he's okay?"

Tank gave me a reassuring smile. "He's fine."

I blew out a breath and moved to the coffee maker. I couldn't explain why I still felt on edge—my ordeal was over and physically, I was back to normal. But I kept experiencing crazy surges of panic, usually accompanied by a certainty that something had gone terribly wrong.

"You feelin' okay?" Tank asked as he opened the refrigerator and pulled out a carton of milk. "No nightmares or anything?"

There it was again—for no logical reason, Tank's innocent question lifted the hair along my arms. What in the world was wrong with me?

"I'm good." I gave Tank a quick smile and was on my way to the table when the front door opened. Brenda came in with her purse on her arm, but instead of a cigarette butt, she carried a piece of paper. Without a word she walked to the dining room table and dropped the paper next to the orb.

We all leaned in for a closer look. Without being told, I knew that something had come over Brenda as she had her morning smoke, and instead of pulling out a cigarette, she had pulled out paper and pen and begun to sketch. The ink had smeared in a few places, but I would have recognized that image if she'd drawn in crayon.

"What is that?" Tank looked from me to the professor, then he grinned at Brenda. "Is this some kind of a joke?"

She pointed to the bottom of her sketch, where she'd drawn leaping flames. "I don't think fire is funny."

The professor and I exchanged a puzzled glance, then I braced my hands on the back of the nearest chair. "Maybe we should have a brainstorming session," I said. "About how our investigation could possibly involve a rubber Gumby."

"Dumby? Who's that?" Tank dropped into a chair at the head of the table, then pulled the box of doughnuts closer and set two glazed, two Boston creams, and a French crueller on a napkin.

Brenda rolled her eyes and sat next to me, eyeing Tank's donut tower while she sipped her coffee.

"Gumby," I said, "used to be a kid's TV show, back in the sixties. I only know about it because Sabba has a DVD collection of old kids' programs. He says he's saving them for my kids because television today is too violent."

"Gumby and his horse Pokey," the professor added, his voice vibrant with nostalgia, "was originally intended to persuade kids to read, but before long the little guy was having independent adventures and leaving the books behind. One of the first attempts at claymation, I suppose. Rudimentary compared to today's standards, but kids from the sixties enjoyed it. As you might imagine, a toy manufacturer licensed the image and sold millions of rubber replicas."

"What I want to know—" Brenda tapped the sketch with the tip of a fingernail—"is why this image popped into my brain. Usually I get an impression that has something to do with a person or an object that ties into our investigation. I don't get this. And I wasn't even born when that show was on TV."

I picked up the sketch and studied it more closely. I envisioned Gumby as being straight or slightly bent at the waist. In my memory he had large oval eyes, a triangle nose, a half-circle mouth, and hyperactive brows that communicated his emotions. But *this* Gumby, if that's really what the image represented, was grotesquely twisted—his mouth appeared to be dripping from his rubber face, his nose was tilted, and his pupils had run into his eyes. And Brenda had drawn flames around his feet . . .

Tank pinned Brenda in a steely gaze. "Are you saying you saw Gumby in hell?"

"No. Yes. I don't know what I saw, but it looked like this." She jabbed the image again. "You know how my sight works—I see, but I don't interpret. I don't want to be wrong."

"Okay." I studied the image again. "So if this is what you saw, why do you think you saw it? After all, we haven't exactly seen any Gumbys running down the street."

"Lemme say it again—I don't interpret. Maybe it's nothing. Maybe I'm confused."

"I'm confused most of the time," Tank said, grinning at her. "But your pictures are always right on."

"Anyone else have an idea?" I looked at the professor, who seemed distracted. His eyes were fixed on the orb, and I was pretty sure he was only half-following the conversation about Brenda's sketch.

"Maybe—" Tank paused to lick sugar off his thumb— "maybe it's a sign."

"Of what?" I asked.

Tank shrugged. "I don't know. But if we see that little rubber dude, we'll know we should pay attention. Gumbo means something."

"Gum*by*," I corrected, "and you're probably right."

"Well, I'm done with this." Brenda stood, cast a longing glance at the doughnuts, then went back to the coffee pot. "Can I suggest that we all get busy? Sittin' around starin' at donuts isn't helping my cravings at all."

"Right," the professor said, pushing away from the table. "Let's get to work."

At lunch, Tank was destroying a mushroom and pineapple pizza when he blurted out the question everyone had been too discreet to ask last night: "By the way, Andi, how was your visit with the shrink yesterday?"

I met his concerned gaze as I took a seat at the dining room table. "Fine. I talked, he talked. He wants me to keep writing in my journal, and he wants to hypnotize me."

Tank's open expression slammed shut. "Not a good idea," he said, his eyes hot. "That kind of stuff is dangerous."

"Actually—" the professor opened a box of spicy chicken wings "—therapeutic hypnosis is nothing like the sideshow theatrics you're undoubtedly thinking of, Tank. Used properly, hypnosis is simply a state of focused concentration. While in a hypnotic trance, a subject is more open to helpful suggestions."

Tank regarded the professor with narrowed eyes. "How can you be sure this doctor won't hurt Andi? He might program her to murder people, or maybe he wants to take advantage of her—"

"Nonsense." The professor waved Tank's concern away. "Some people can't even be hypnotized, and no one under hypnosis can be forced to do anything he or she wouldn't ordinarily do. Andi would certainly be safe from any predacious doctor."

"Unless she don't want to be." Brenda grinned at me. "You gotta admit, that man is *fine*. He wouldn't have to use hypnosis to get some lovin' from me."

"I'm not in the market for love." I shot an equal opportunity glare around the table. "I just want those voices out of my head—for good." I looked at the professor, who had also been infected with the fungus. "Have you noticed anything odd about your thoughts? Have you heard any *echoes* of those voices?"

"No." The professor gave me a sympathetic smile. "But I wasn't infected nearly as long as you."

"That's it, then." I grabbed a slice of pizza. "I have another appointment tomorrow, and I'm going to tell Drummond to start swinging his watch, or whatever he does to hypnotize people."

"I second the motion," the professor said.

"I third it," Brenda added.

Tank growled. "My opinion may not matter much, but I'm against it."

Daniel, who had been plucking the mushrooms from his pizza, lifted his hand, signaling his agreement with Tank.

I sighed. I would have liked to have unanimous support, but three-to-two was still a win.

After lunch, I went back to the dining room and opened the cardboard box on the floor. The orb lay beneath the dishtowel I'd thrown over it, so I grabbed it, dishcloth and all, and set it on the table. I found my tablet, my tape measure, and a pen, then pulled the dishtowel away from the orb . . . and gasped.

The orb had changed again. Instead of being silver or gold, the orb's surface was covered with rows of trapezoids . . . and in each four-sided shape I saw the stage, the woman, and the basket from my recurrent nightmare.

My first instinct was to cover the orb and run. The thing knew too much. It was either reading my mind or it had invaded my dreams, but in either case, it was an intruder.

But maybe I only *thought* I was seeing those things. Maybe I was imprinting those little shapes on the orb; maybe someone else would see something different.

I glanced into the living room. Brenda had curled up on the couch and Daniel was sitting on the floor playing *Battleship Megadeath*. Fortunately, we had convinced him not to target any of *our* ships during the day, so none of our phones erupted in sirens and horns while we were working. But occasionally we heard MEGADEATH APPROACHING, CAPTAIN. DEFEND YOUR BATTLESHIP over the sound of wailing sirens and knew that Daniel's ship was in peril.

Fortunately, the more he played, the better he became. Which meant fewer interruptions for us.

I threw the dishtowel over the orb again. "Hey, guys. Will you come here a minute? I want to try a little experiment."

Brenda and Daniel looked at me, then Brenda sighed and swung her legs to the floor. "Come on, kiddo," she said. "It's always good to take a break."

They pulled out chairs, sat, and waited.

"I'm going to lift this cloth," I told them, "and I want you to describe the orb."

"Okay," Brenda said. Daniel simply placed his arms on the table, then propped his chin on his hands.

"Okay—here goes."

I yanked the cloth away in one quick motion. Instead the puzzlement and confusion I expected to see on their faces, I saw nothing but calm curiosity.

"Blue," Brenda said, smiling. "Kinda reminds me of Planet Earth."

"Pretty," Daniel said, his eyes wide with wonder.

I turned to look at the orb—it *was* blue, a deep, metallic color that shone like a new car. No trapezoids, no images, no nightmares. Which meant either the orb had changed, or I was losing touch with reality.

Brenda lifted a brow. "Is that what you wanted us to say? Or did you want me to call it something fancy like *sapphire*?

I forced a smile. "Nope, it's blue. That's all I needed."

Brenda shook her head slightly, then squeezed Daniel's shoulder. "Whaddya say to an ice cream? I think the professor has some cones stashed away in the pantry."

I pulled out my tape measure and scale, trying to behave as though nothing out of the ordinary had happened. But when I measured the orb and found that it had expanded *another* inch, I sat back and stared at the thing. The orb was getting bigger, any one could see that. But how?

Even more important, why?

Chapter 7

Tuesday dawned clear, hot, and blue. Brenda woke up grumpy and with a headache, so the professor suggested that she take Daniel to the beach for a few hours. "Just stay out of trouble," he warned. "Tank, why don't you go with her and the kid?"

Tank hesitated. "What about you, Andi? Want to come with us?"

I pulled my laptop closer. "I'm gonna do some research, then I'm supposed to see Dr. D. You guys go on without me."

Tank didn't look very happy, but Brenda and Daniel did. So off they went.

Once they'd gone, the professor stretched out in the worn easy chair and kept working through the box of documents from the clipping service. "I know there's something in here," he said, pushing his reading glasses up the bridge of his nose. "I'm just afraid we won't recognize it when we see it." He glanced at me. "How are you coming with the orb?"

I blew out a breath. "It's pretty freaky. It changes. It expands and contracts. It seems to have consciousness."

"We need facts and evidence," the professor said. "You know the principles of scientific investigation. Hunches and appearances can be wrong."

"I'm working on it," I told him. "But more important, so are the boys in the basement."

The professor smiled and went back to his reading.

My reference to the boys in the basement was sort of an inside joke. The professor spoke of *the boys* often when we first started working together—his way of teaching me that during an investigation, everything we saw, heard, and experienced was stored in the subconscious until the *boys* made the necessary connections and provided the conscious mind with an answer to the problem.

I needed my subconscious to put in some serious overtime because lately my *conscious* mind had been seriously messed up.

I removed the dishcloth over the orb to view the thing's latest incarnation. The orb's color had shifted; the blue color now had a greenish tinge. And it may have grown, but I wasn't in the mood to take measurements. I was ready to get my head straightened out first.

I called Dr. Drummond's cell phone, and felt a flutter of nerves when he actually answered. "This is Andi," I said. "And I'm ready to be hypnotized."

Silence rolled over the phone line for a moment, then he chuckled. "All right, let's move ahead. But I'm not at the office today—I'm at the condo, so I'll need to text you the address."

"A condo?" I frowned. Meeting a doctor at his home didn't seem very professional, but then again, he wasn't in full-time practice here. He was doing me a favor by agreeing to see me at all. "Where is the condo?"

"Clearwater Beach," he said. "I think you'll like the view. Anyway, we'll talk, I'll hypnotize you, and then I'll let you enjoy the rest of your afternoon. Oh—and you'll get to meet my mother. Lucky you."

I relaxed at the mention of his mom. "I'll be there in half an hour. Thanks."

I couldn't help smiling as I drove north to Clearwater Beach. Though my sleeping hours had been filled with nightmares, the bright sunshine and wide blue sky evaporated my feelings of dread. The doctor was staying in a condo at Sand Key, a nice development that appealed to tourists and snowbirds.

I parked the car and smiled at several sunburned and sandaled tourists as I got into the elevator and rode up to the fifteenth floor.

When Dr. Drummond answered the door, I entered a bit timidly. I knew the professor would have a fit if he knew I was meeting the doctor in his condo, but when I followed Drummond from the foyer into a living room, I was relieved to see an older woman—his mother, I presumed—seated on the sofa. She was reading the newspaper, but after welcoming me and apologizing for her casual appearance, she gathered up the pages and headed into the kitchen.

"My mother," Dr. Drummond said, watching her go. "She loves Florida, so I insisted she come along on this trip. She's going to hate going back to Edinburgh."

I smiled and moved into the middle of the living room. "Does it matter where I sit?"

"Sit anywhere you like." Dr. Drummond waited until I sat at the end of the sofa, then he took the nearest chair. "Have you been writing in your journal?"

"I have. Every day."

"Did you write about your feelings after the latest nightmare? Are you recording all the details?"

"As many as I can remember."

"Good." He gave me an approving smile. "All right. What we are going to do now is play a game of 'let's pretend.' You are going to pretend to follow my instructions and fall into a trance. You are going to let your mind go as blank as possible, and you're going to let your face relax. Don't react to anything I say or do, but listen to my suggestions and focus on my voice. Take a deep breath in and slowly release it. That's right. Do it again—inhale and exhale, deeper and deeper. You're going to go deeper and deeper, you're going to become more and more still. Watch me. Look into my eyes."

I listened. I watched until my head grew heavy and I felt like I was staring *through* Hamish Drummond, like I could almost tumble forward and fall through the man into another dimension. Or one of the professor's multiverses.

"When I count to five," Drummond went on, his voice flat and steady, "you will become more and more aware of the room around you. I am going to count, and by the time I reach five, you will look up and feel refreshed, alert, and fantastic. You will not have that dream tonight. You will not hear voices in your head. Never again. Ready? One . . . Two . . . Three . . . Four . . . Five."

I lifted my head and looked around. Hamish sat on a chair in front of me, smiling expectantly, and from the kitchen I heard the sounds of clanging pots and pans. "So?" I asked. "Are we going to do the hypnosis now?"

His smile broadened. "My dear girl. We've already finished."

I looked at my hands, the room, and the clock—I had left the rental house at 10:00 a.m., but the clock had moved to 11:15. The drive must have taken longer than I realized.

I smiled in a flood of relief. "It didn't work, did it?"

"But it did."

"What? I don't feel any different. I mean—I feel fine, but I'm nearly always fine when I'm awake. The nightmares begin after I go to sleep. "

I waited for his response, but he had lowered his gaze and seemed to be smiling on a spot on the carpet. "Hamish?" I tried again. "Did you hear me?"

He lifted his head, then he reached out and took my hand. "What did you just call me?"

I opened my mouth, ready to say *Dr. Drummond*, but my spoken words were still vibrating on the air. I'd called him *Hamish*. And I never, *ever* called professionals by their first names.

My jaw dropped, and the doctor squeezed my hand. "Nice to meet you, too, Andi. I hope you wilna mind being on a first-name basis."

"How—why—how did you do that?"

He lifted one shoulder in a shrug. "I simply made the hypnotic suggestion that we call each other by our Christian names. Your subconscious agreed that it was a good idea."

"But—but—"

He held up a restraining hand. "Don't worry about it; you can call me anything you like. But how do you *feel?* How do you feel about your nightmares?"

I halted, then closed my eyes to evaluate the feelings of dread and anxiety that had been simmering in my brain over the past several days. I felt nothing . . . but clarity. The anxiety and fear had vanished.

I opened my eyes and gave him the first genuine smile I'd mustered in days. "Hamish—Dr. Drummond—right now I think I could kiss you."

He grinned, then stood. "I'd better let you go. I'm sure your friends are wondering where you are."

I stood, too. "The professor gave us the morning off. Something about all work and no play—"

"Why don't you stay for lunch? I'm supposed to barbecue a stack of spare ribs or some such thing, and Mother's made a Clootie dumpling for dessert. We'd love the company."

I laughed. "A Clootie *what?*"

"Stay . . . and you'll see."

I looked away and bit my lip, wondering if he'd done any hypnotic hocus pocus to evoke the glorious feeling of happiness that was bubbling up inside me. But even if he had, why should I mind?

I turned to face him, then hugged my arms and nodded. "I'd love to stay for lunch."

I didn't return to Ghostbusters Central until mid-afternoon. My bright mood dimmed when I came through the door and found Tank scowling at me. "We've been worried sick," he said, flushing. "Where have you been?"

I lifted both brows, then glanced around the room to see if any of the others were as upset as Tank. The professor was peering at me from above his readers, and Brenda had stopped reading a press clipping to look at me with a question on her face. But Daniel was deep into his *Battleship Megadeath* game and didn't even look up.

"I went to my appointment," I said, forcing myself to remain calm. "And then Hamish—Dr. Drummond—invited me to have lunch with him and his mother. We ate. We talked. And that was it."

I tossed my purse onto the coffee table and strode to the dining room, where the orb waited under the dishtowel. Tank could stew if he wanted to, but I'd done nothing wrong and I refused to get caught up in his fears. I hadn't asked him to worry about me, and I wouldn't. Ever.

Dear Journal:

After coming in from lunch, I sat down, took my equipment from the cardboard box, then pulled the dishcloth from the orb. The sphere had taken on a pink tone, and seemed to be vibrating slightly. I placed my fingertips on it and closed my eyes, trying to discern whether the humming sound came from the orb or some other mechanism in the house . . .

The sound faded, and I felt no vibration under my fingertips. I pulled out the tape measure and wrapped it around the widest part of the sphere: eighteen inches.

I whistled and made a note on my tablet. Heat caused objects to expand, but I hadn't noticed a significant elevation in temperature. Had the dishcloth trapped heat beneath its surface? Or had direct window light fallen on the orb during the early afternoon?

I picked up my digital scale and set it on the table. I then slid my hand beneath the base of the orb and prepared to gently roll it onto the scale. But no sooner had I lifted the orb than it floated out of my hand, hovering above my palm.

I couldn't move. Had the orb floated because the momentum of my hand propelled it upward? Or had it risen under its own power?

"Professor," I called, making every effort to keep calm. "Can you come over here?"

I heard the creak of his easy chair, then McKinney appeared in the doorway. "What—ah!"

He stared, too, and a moment later Tank, Brenda, and Daniel joined him in the opening to the dining room. The orb had not moved—it remained about two inches above my palm, not spinning, not vibrating, just . . . waiting.

Obeying an impulse, I lowered my open hand and the orb descended with it, but maintained that two-inch distance. I lifted my hand, moved it left, right, and with each movement, the orb traveled with me.

"Fascinating," the professor whispered, crossing one arm over his chest. "Like a baby bird that's imprinted on its mother."

I snorted. "I hardly think that's the case. It's not alive. It lacks even the potential for life—"

Without warning, the orb left my palm and flew toward my face, astounding me with its speed and forcefulness. I threw up my hands and ducked reflexively, but the orb stopped short of striking me. It hung in the empty air in front of my eyes, then zipped off toward the professor, where it hung before him, almost as though it were taunting him . . .

Perhaps the orb was more than I thought.

Tank sputtered in amazement, and the orb flew to him, hovering a half inch in front of his nose. When Brenda laughed, the orb flew toward her, then remained tantalizingly out of reach when she tried to catch it. It zipped left and right, up and down, making a game of her spirited attempts to touch the thing.

Meanwhile, the professor kept his gazed fixed to it, his eyes narrow with calculation.

Tank and Brenda had made a game of it, an odd sort of chase through the living room, with the orb spinning high and low. It hovered near the ceiling, then it ducked beneath a shelf in the bookcase. Daniel put down his phone as they played, and though his eyes followed Tank's and Brenda's clumsy moves, he did not smile.

"What do you think?" the professor said, coming toward me. "Benign or malevolent?"

I shook my head. "Can't tell. But considering where it originated, I don't think I'd leave that thing out at night."

"So where do we put it?"

I glanced around the kitchen. We had a basic supply of pots and pans, a grill on the back porch, and three or four closets. I didn't know what to do with the orb, but I didn't want it to fly away . . .

"Ah!" I ran through the utility room and stepped onto a shabby little patio where the previous owner had left a pile of odds and ends. One of those was a rusty birdcage, and it would be perfect for the orb.

I carried the old birdcage into the house, then removed the plastic bottom, leaving the cage open at the base. "All right, Tank, Brenda," I called. "Unless you want to sleep with that thing hovering overhead tonight, you'd better help me capture it."

Until that moment they'd been playing with it, then Tank got serious. He grabbed Brenda's sweater from the back of a chair and held it open, then chased the orb until it hovered over the dining room table. I could have sworn it was looking at me when Tank crept up from behind and threw the sweater over it. Together, we transferred it to the bottom of the birdcage, then I snapped the wire section into place.

We stood back, and I suddenly realized how silly we looked—four adults and a kid staring at a shiny blue-green ball in a rusty birdcage. The orb did not hover or fly or protest, but simply sat on the plastic floor amid traces of old paint and bird droppings.

But it wouldn't buzz around our heads tonight.

I woke at 2:00 a.m., not because I'd had a bad dream, but because the boys in the basement were pounding on the plumbing, desperate to give me a new idea. I padded through and into the dining room, then clicked on the light. The orb sat motionless in the bottom of the birdcage, but I had plans for it . . .

I pulled out my tools—measuring tape, drill, protective eyewear. Then I let myself out of the house and went out to my car, quietly opening the trunk and removing the case I'd tossed in on a hunch—the microscope I'd used for a science fair in high school. It wasn't the most powerful model, but it might be strong enough to verify the new hypothesis.

Back inside the house, I set up the microscope and removed the wire portion of the birdcage. Then I slipped a clean sheet of paper beneath the orb. Keeping my left hand on the sphere lest it try to zip away, I picked up the drill and turned it on, scraping the bit over the orb's surface as I had before. The drill bit made only a slight indentation, but I didn't care about marking it—any scratch would soon disappear, anyway.

I set the drill down and quickly brought the wire cage back over the orb, then slipped my left hand free. Once the orb was secure, I used a pair of kitchen tongs to slide the sheet of paper through the bottom opening and onto the table.

Working quickly, I put a drop of water on an empty slide, then sprinkled the water droplet with tiny metallic shavings from the orb.

"What on earth are you doing? I thought you were a burglar."

I startled, then glanced over my shoulder at the professor, who stood in the open doorway with a pistol in his hand.

"Where did you get *that*? And why are you pointing it at me?"

"I'm not pointing it at you. And I picked it up two days ago because I thought it might prove useful in saving our collective bacon."

The professor set the weapon on the counter, then came forward to watch me work. I dropped the coverslip onto the shavings in water, then set the slide on the stage and dialed in the magnification. Then I focused.

I had expected to see metallic strands, bars, whatever—but I saw patterns. Clear, unmistakable, and organized. *Cells.* Not the typical cells with a nucleus, a cell membrane, and cytoplasm, but cells nonetheless. Even with my puny home microscope I could make out cell walls and a dot that might be a nucleus or other mechanism for controlling cell development. Furthermore, I saw the sort of asymmetry that was common in living cells . . .

Goosebumps pebbled my flesh as I looked at the

professor. "It's not a machine," I whispered. "It's alive."

Light bulbs were going off in my head, and I wanted to shout. The real me was back. For the first time in weeks I felt excitement sparking in my veins. I was seeing patterns, putting ideas together, and hearing that satisfying *click* that meant my instincts were right.

"Impossible." The professor sat and pulled the microscope toward him, straining the power cord. "All life is carbon-based. This is metal and wire and circuits—"

"It may *contain* metal and wires and circuits," I said, my words coming out in double-time, "but it's not expanding and contracting, it's growing. It's healing itself. It's replicating and repairing damaged cells. It's organized. It uses energy. It responds to its environment. All we have left to determine—"

The professor lifted his head from the eyepiece. "Is what?"

"If it can reproduce."

The professor leaned back in his chair and thrust his hands into the pockets of his robe. "Impossible."

"You can say that all night long," I told him, "but it doesn't change what you see in that microscope. What we've seen over the last few days. Whoever made this orb—"

"The Gate?"

"Whoever made it has access to technology far beyond conventional research. This thing, this living metal, could be derived from an alien culture. It could have come from another galaxy. It could be so advanced that not even our government knows about it—"

"But *we* do? This makes no sense." He leaned forward and touched my arm. "I know you're flush with excitement right now, but reality's going to hit you in the morning. As far as I know, no one has ever found a non-carbon based life form. In the entire universe, Andi. No one. Nowhere."

He stood, nodded, and turned toward the hallway. "I'm going back to bed now. And in the morning I'm going to come in here and tell you that I had the oddest dream. And you're going to laugh and give me a cup of coffee, and we're going to go back to reading and searching for needles in haystacks. So goodnight."

"Fine. Just take the gun with you."

I watched him pick up the pistol and shuffle away, and I knew his mind needed time to accept the impossible, the improbable, and the nonexistent. But by tomorrow, the boys in the basement would have done their work and he'd come around.

He always did.

Chapter 8

      I slept late the next morning, and might have slept even longer if not for the noise coming from the living room. I threw on a robe and stumbled down the hallway, then went instantly awake when I saw who stood next to Brenda: Dr. Hamish Drummond, and he was anything but calm. His face was red from exertion, his forehead was damp with sweat, and he was leaning over the coffee table, eye to eye with the professor.

      "What's going on?" I pushed a tangle of curls away from my face to better see them.

      Tank, who'd been blocked from view by a wall, stepped into my field of vision. "Your doctor friend says he's been visited by one of the orbs."

      "What?" Ghost spiders danced over my spine. "Why?"

I stepped around Tank to see the doctor. "Why would the orbs visit you?"

"I don't know, and that's why I'm here." Hamish looked from me to the professor. "Tell me what you know about the people controlling those things."

"We don't know anything." The professor crossed his arms. "We aren't even sure what the orbs are used for."

I knew better—we knew the orbs were used for spying and for destroying the green fungus when it got out of control. I knew the orbs were made of living metal. But apparently the professor didn't want to share what we had learned.

I pressed my lips together as another thought made my stomach twist. Did Hamish know the professor was lying? He might, if I had told him what we'd learned about the orbs. I had no idea what I'd said under hypnosis.

Hamish regarded the professor with a skeptical gaze, then nodded. "I see," he said, a cryptic response that could have meant anything.

Brenda leaned against the wall. "Why don't you tell us what you saw?" she suggested, an easy smile playing on her lips.

Hamish looked from her to me, then he slipped his hands into his pockets. "I went to the office this morning. The air smelled different, and the room was unusually warm, so I checked and found a shattered window. I immediately turned to see if anything was missing. That's when I saw the thing. It had been hiding in a corner, and when I spotted it, it flew straight at me. I ducked, then it flew out the window and I lost track of it."

All of us looked at each other. His description of the orb's behavior seemed accurate, but I knew the professor would be skeptical.

"Which brings us back to why," Brenda said, twiddling her unsmoked cigarette between her fingers. "Why would an orb be spying on *you*?"

"And that's why I'm here." Hamish folded his arms.

"I'd never seen anything like that until I met the five of you. I wouldn't know what it was if Andi hadn't told me."

There it was—the finger of blame, pointed squarely at me.

"I'm sorry," I said, giving him an apologetic look. "I hate that I've gotten you involved in all this. If you want to stop seeing me, I'll understand. I *am* feeling better."

The professor had narrowed his eyes at the beginning of Hamish's story, now he nodded. "All right, then. I think we can assume that whoever might be interested in us is also interested in the doctor. They're probably conducting damage control. We know about their experimentation with the fungus and we know that it could easily be weaponized."

"But why?" Hamish lifted both brows. "It doesna make sense. Why would they want a weapon? Why would they kill thousands of innocent people? What's the end game?"

I had no answer, and I didn't think the professor did, either. Brenda gave the professor a *what-next* look, and Tank scratched his head.

"We don't know what the end game is," I said, speaking up because I felt responsible. "But we do know that the things we've seen do not bode well for anyone."

Hamish tipped back his head and looked at me, then he nodded. "I guess I'll just have to move on and forget about it . . . if I can."

"Sorry," I said again. "I never dreamed they'd come after you."

"Let this be a lesson to you, lass," he answered, his mouth curving in a half-smile. "Be careful who you tell your secrets to."

"I'll walk you to the door," I said. "Sorry about not being awake when you came in. I was up late last night."

He walked with me through the doorway, then lingered outside on the tiny front porch. Aware that I was outside in my robe with no makeup, I cinched my robe tighter and folded my arms, waiting to hear whatever he wanted to say.

"Thanks for stayin' for lunch yesterday," he said. "My mother enjoyed meeting you."

I looked down and smiled. "I enjoyed meeting her. It was nice to get away—" I gestured to the house behind me "—from all this. But if you want to read my journals, maybe to learn a little more about what we've been doing, I'd be happy to let you see them."

He shook his head. "I never read my patients' private thoughts. I said that wee notebook was for your eyes alone, and I meant it. But—" he wagged a finger at me, "I might have to seriously consider turning you over to another doctor. It's unethical, you understand, for a doctor to see a patient to whom he's personally attracted."

I stared as the words slowly sank in. Did he mean what I thought he meant? Was he really attracted to me? I liked him, but then again, who wouldn't? He was handsome, charming, intelligent, and who could resist that accent?

"I'd better be goin'." Hamish stepped off the porch and waved, then opened the door of his convertible.

"Nice car," I called, coming down the stairs.

"A rental." He grinned. "But I'm enjoyin' it for as long as I'm in Florida. Might as well go back home with a tan."

I laughed and stepped closer. The interior was what I expected to see in a new sports car—leather seats, power everything, burled wood in the dash—then I spied something so unexpected I froze. On the dashboard, sitting like a tiny little person, was a green Gumby.

I widened my eyes and pointed. "What . . . is . . . that?"

He followed my finger, then grinned. "You mean Gumby?"

"Why do you have a Gumby in your car?"

He chuckled. "'Tis my brother's stand-in. He gave it to me when I left home. Said he wanted to come to America, but since he couldn't, Gumby would have to stand in for him." He tilted his head. "Does that mean something? You look like you've seen a ghost."

I drew a deep breath and felt my shoulders relax. Surely the Gumby was harmless—so why had Brenda sketched him?

"It's cute," I said, stepping away from the car. "But I'd better let you go. I'm sure you have work to do."

"Nothing more interesting than talking to you," he said, sliding into the driver's seat. "But seriously—call if you need to see me. You have my number."

I nodded and backed away, then watched him pull out of the drive and head north. And as the convertible merged into traffic at the intersection, another random thought struck: how had he known where to find us?

I must have given him the address while under hypnosis.

Inside the house, I discovered that Hamish Drummond's arrival had drastically affected my friend's moods. Tank wore a decidedly worried expression. Brenda kept grinning at me, probably delighted by the thought of observing a trans-Atlantic fling, and the professor radiated disapproval, undoubtedly because he thought I had crossed the line between personal and professional relationships. The only one who seemed unaffected was Daniel, who sat on the floor drawing pictures while he listened for sounds of distress from his battleships.

"He's a good doctor," I finally said, breaking the tense silence that had reigned ever since I came through the doorway, "and a nice guy. But that's the extent of our relationship."

"Good thing," Tank said. "I was wondering if he made up that orb story just to—you know."

The professor removed his glasses and pinched the bridge of his nose. "I don't understand why an orb would enter his office—no logic in that. He hasn't been in contact with the fungus. And he knows nothing about our work aside from what he's learned from Andi. Which brings up something else—" He shifted his gaze to me. "Maybe it's not a good idea for him to hypnotize you again. You could tell him far too much."

Tank's brow furrowed. "I'm not following you."

"Andi will explain the latest developments later. But it's not logical to have a spybot, if you want to call it that, follow someone with secondhand information if the primary source is available. If the Gate wanted to spy on us, it'd be more logical for them to have an orb follow Andi."

I closed my eyes, thinking of the orb in the birdcage. What if the thing had been abandoned on purpose? It had been with us for days, so it had seen and heard all kinds of things . . .

"What . . . if . . ." Brenda spoke slowly, as if easing into her thoughts—"the dark powers of the Gate have somehow been drawn to the doctor through Andi? I mean, he was just one of seven billion people on the planet until Andi became his patient. But he's a bright guy, he's from Europe, and who knows how many people he has the potential to reach. If they wanted pets to carry the fungus to humans, why wouldn't they want a guy from Scotland to carry it overseas?"

The professor brought his finger to his lip. "That's a surprisingly logical thought, Barnick. If the Gate started their work with the fungus here, they might want Dr. Drummond to carry a more polished specimen to Europe. If he could be exposed through Andi—"

"But that's not possible because the fungus is gone. I don't have it any more." I gave the professor a warning look. "Can we drop this discussion and get back to work?" When no one objected, I turned to Brenda. "By the way, I've spotted Gumby. Dr. Drummond drives with one on the dashboard of his car."

Brenda's mouth opened and closed, like a fish gasping for air. "You're kidding."

"What does that have to do with anything?" Tank

asked. "I don't think we should be involving a guy who—"

"Wait. The figure in Barnick's sketch—" The professor reached for his briefcase, then shuffled papers. "Here it is. *This* Gumby is twisted and mangled. Did Drummond's look like this?"

"No. His Gumby looked like Mr. Universe compared to that one."

"Then what you saw *isn't* what Barnick saw. I must admit that it's an improbable coincidence, but the images don't match. So let's move on."

I sighed and pushed hair out of my eyes. "Moving on, then. If you could all join me in the dining room—"

"Guys?" The alarmed note in Brenda's voice lifted the hairs on my arms. I turned to see her holding one of Daniel's drawings. "I think you should all see this."

Tank and the professor joined me near the sofa. In the typical style of a ten-year-old, Daniel had drawn the image of Hamish Drummond, identifiable by his black hair, dark pants, and white shirt. He stood behind a flat two-dimensional table, but behind the doctor, on the wall, Daniel had drawn three frowning shadow creatures.

The sight of them gave me the willies.

"Daniel," Brenda asked, smiling gently. "Who are these people?"

Daniel glanced at the picture, then shrugged.

"Did you see them?"

He nodded.

"Are they, um—" Brenda struggled for the right word "—bad?"

Daniel shook his head. "No duch."

"Are they good? Like the invisible guy who hangs out with you sometimes?"

Daniel shook his head again. "No anioł."

"So you don't know who they are?"

This time he lifted his head and met Brenda's gaze straight on. "I don't know," he said, his eyes welling with tears. "I don't."

Brenda smiled. "That's okay, kid."

She consoled Daniel as the professor, Tank, and I tiptoed into the dining room for a quiet conference. "We know he sees supernatural beings," I said, establishing known territory. "We know he's seen evil manifestations—"

"And angels," Tank interrupted. "At least, that's what I think they are."

"But he's never been uncertain about what he sees . . . until now."

The professor scratched at his stubbled chin. "Maybe they aren't manifestations. Maybe he's exercising artistic license."

Tank guffawed. "He's never done that before."

"He's ten," the professor pointed out. "Every day he does something he's never done before."

"Maybe they're a kind of spirit he's never met," I suggested. "Aren't supernatural beings sorted into classes? After all, the angels have cherubim and seraphim and archangels . . . "

As one, we turned and studied the boy, who was drawing another picture. "If some kind of dark force is following Hamish because of me," I whispered, "I—we— have to help him find a way to be free."

I made my big announcement after I'd placed the orb cage in the utility room where it couldn't listen to our conversation. I don't know if it heard things—could it possibly have some sort of auditory mechanism?—but I didn't want to take a chance.

The professor didn't react to my news; he simply took another sip of his coffee and set his mug back on the table. Brenda and Tank stared at me with puzzled looks—they knew I'd stumbled onto something big, but they couldn't quite grasp the significance. But they would soon enough.

Daniel only looked up at me, smiled, and went back to

drawing his pictures.

"So," I said, crossing my arms and settling back in my chair, "this is huge news, and it might actually help us locate the Gate."

"How's that?" Brenda's frown deepened. "You've lost me."

"I was lost at 'I've had a breakthrough,'" Tank said, grinning. "Why don't you start over?"

"The orb," I said slowly, "is made of living material. You've seen it expand and contract—it's actually been growing and shrinking. It has healed its injuries. You've seen it fly purposefully. For all I know it may be transmitting information to its creators."

"Is that why it's in the utility room?" Brenda said. "You think it's a spy?"

I shrugged. "I suspect that it was told—or commanded or programmed—to watch over Dr. Mathis, which it did until Tank smashed it in the lab. Now that it's had time to heal, it may not have a command to follow. It may be waiting. It may be looking for an opportunity to escape and go back to its programmer or whatever. Its creator."

"You think someone created this?" The professor narrowed his eyes, but at least he had begun to consider my hypothesis. "Last night you were talking about aliens."

"We can't rule that out," I said, "because as you pointed out last night, no one has ever found anything like this in nature. Maybe it's a machine-human hybrid."

"Whoa." Tank held up both hands in a defensive posture. "Now you're talkin' Terminators One, Two, and Three."

I blew out a breath. "Science fiction gets a lot of stuff right. But the orb—" I pointed toward the utility room "—is a living thing. So we have to treat it as such."

"How is this supposed to help us find the Gate?" These late developments must have shaken Brenda, because she had popped her unlit cigarette into her mouth. "Don't tell me you want to let it go and see where it lands."

"No—but that's not a bad idea, if we could find a tracking device." I lifted a brow. "I was thinking about money. If you were a secret organization and you came up with an amazing and totally unique substance like living metal, what would you do with it?"

"Sell it," Tank said. "You'd want to make a lot of money."

"Control it." Brenda tapped her nails on the tabletop. "You wouldn't want your secrets to get out. You'd guard them. Watch out for industrial espionage and that kind of thing."

"I'd patent it," the professor added. "If it's an actual life form, or even a hybrid, you'd patent the process and the result."

"Yes, yes, and yes." I grinned at all of them. "And wow, is it ever good to be back. I feel like my brain is finally working at full power."

"So God bless the shrink," Brenda said. "Get back to the topic at hand."

"Okay." I pressed my hands to the table. "Professor, why don't you check the U.S. Patent office and see if anyone has applied for a patent on living metal or some similar term. Brenda, start searching for stock tips, new companies, anything you can find about living metal. And Tank, if someone claims to have invented living metal, see if you can find any mentions of how the substance could be used. If we follow these threads, they'll lead us to the Gate . . . or at least to one of their shell companies."

Brenda squinted at me. "Say again?"

"Think of the Gate as the big, bulbous head of an octopus," I said, "with long tentacles to represent the different shell companies, organizations, schools, whatever. The offshoots may carry on legitimate business, but the head controls them all. If we can find even a few names associated with one of these branch groups, we'll have the names of people who are either part of the Gate, or loosely associated with them."

Brenda blew out a breath. "Sounds a lot easier than lookin' through all those boxes of clippings."

"One question—" Tank held up his hand. "Does this mean we have to watch what we say around the orb? And if that thing's really alive, maybe we should make it more comfortable. I hate to think of it all cooped up in that rusty cage."

"Let Andi keep it with her," Brenda said, standing. "She's its mother."

They laughed and left the table, leaving me to wonder if they could possibly be right.

By the end of the day we had made solid progress. The professor reported that no one had applied for a "living metal" patent in the United States, but Tank found a researcher who had created metal cells capable of reproduction. "Dude's from the University of Glasgow," Tank said, consulting a computer printout, "and he calls them iCHELLS." He lowered the paper. "Basically, he took a lot of metal atoms and mixed them in a solution. I don't understand all the details, but positive ions bonded with negative ions and such. He says he can design the cells to do certain things." He slid the paper toward me. "More details in the article, if you want to read it."

"Thanks, Tank." I set the article aside and bit my lip. The University of Glasgow . . . Scotland. Dr. Drummond was from Scotland, too—coincidence?

"I found a company." Brenda turned her laptop around and showed me the website, a basic design of not much more than a logo and lots of text. "Summit Biotechnologies. They're small, but they're ramping up. I found some stockbroker sites that were raving about a potential IPO in the next year or two."

Tank squinched his face into a question. "What's—"

"Initial public offering," the professor said. "They want

to sell stock on the New York Stock Exchange."

"That's cool." I looked around the circle, hoping my excitement was contagious. "Tomorrow, let's investigate Summit Biotechnologies. Maybe we should take a trip to their office and nose around to see what we can find."

"I hope they're in a big city," Brenda said, pulling a pack of cigarettes from her purse. "Maybe New York or Paris. If we have to do some globe-trotting, let's trot in nice places, okay?"

The rest of us split up and headed to our rooms. I felt tired and happy, and I knew I'd sleep like a rock. Now that Hamish had taken care of my nightmares, I was looking forward to a good sleep.

I pulled out my journal and tapped the cover, wondering if I really needed to keep writing in it. I was feeling so much better . . . but what was the harm? It felt good to write about everything that had happened, and for once I had good news to report.

After putting my journal away, I crawled into bed and was asleep before my head hit the pillow.

I was dreaming that I was a glamorous World War II spy, wearing a trench coat and secretly taking pictures of important documents, when Brenda shook me awake.

"Hey." She was in pajamas and leaning over me, a shadowy figure in the dark.

"What?" I blinked the remnants of my dream away as my eyes adjusted. "Brenda. What's up?"

"I was about to ask you the same question."

"Huh?" I rose onto my elbows and looked around. "What do you mean?"

She gave me an odd look, then sat on the edge of her bed. "A few minutes ago," she said, "you got out of bed, walked to the desk, and used your phone to take pictures of your journal. Then you crawled back into your bed and went back to sleep." She tilted her head. "Why'd you do that?"

Curiosity brought me fully awake. "You must have

been dreaming."

"I haven't been to bed yet."

Frowning, I got out of bed and walked to the little desk in our bedroom. My journal lay in the corner, right where I'd placed it before going to sleep. My phone lay on the desk, too, and when I unlocked it and checked my photos, I saw only pictures of Abby, the beach, and a few I'd taken of Daniel.

I held up the phone so Brenda could see it. "No photos."

"Maybe you deleted 'em. You stood there for a couple of minutes before you went back to sleep."

"Why would I do that? Who would I send pictures to?"

Brenda folded her arms. "Good questions."

"Here's another one—why did you watch me do all that before asking what I was doing?"

Brenda snorted. "Haven't you ever heard that it's dangerous to wake a sleepwalker? I called to you a couple of times, but when you didn't answer, I thought you might be sleepwalkin'. So I decided to wait and make sure you didn't hurt yourself."

"I'm not a sleepwalker. I've *never* been a sleepwalker."

I sat on the bed and checked everything I knew to check—nothing odd in recent phone calls, nothing in text messages, nothing unusual in my emails. My address book was open to the page with Hamish Drummond's phone number, but I had called him the other day.

Sighing, I tossed the phone on the desk. "I think you were dreaming."

Brenda opened her mouth, and I knew she wanted to say I was crazy.

But instead she clamped her mouth shut, got into bed, and turned her back to me.

Chapter 9

By the time I got up Thursday morning, Brenda and Tank were involved in a spirited discussion of what might be possible with living metal—"A robot that looks human and makes its food through photosynthesis!" Brenda said, to which Tank countered, "Terminator Ten!"

The professor had his laptop open at the counter and was reading a long email. I was slipping past him to pour a cup of coffee when he caught my eye and pointed to the screen. "Our marching orders," he said. "We're to stay here until we receive plane tickets via messenger. We'll be leaving in a day or two."

"And goin' where?" Brenda wanted to know. "Can I vote for Paris?"

I slid into the chair next to the professor. "I don't

know who these people are," I said, speaking of the mysterious benefactors who occasionally provided tickets, visas, and other things we needed for travel, "but I'm glad they're on our side."

"Why don't we put a little effort into figuring out who they are?" Brenda asked, casually stealing marshmallows from Daniel's bowl of Lucky Charms. "Or would that be too much like lookin' a gift horse in the mouth?"

"I'm just happy knowing the good guys have a team." Tank smiled above the rim of his coffee mug. "I'd hate to think that we were standing up to the Gate alone."

"If these people want us to know who they are, I trust they'll tell us," the professor said, closing his laptop. "In the mean time, we do occasionally run into others. Like Little Foot. The nun. And that crazy taxi driver in Rome."

I tapped the professor's arm. "Since we'll be leaving soon, I think I'll run some errands this morning and maybe stop at my grandparents' house," I said. "I'll try to be back by lunch time."

After showering and dressing, I picked up my purse, finger-combed my hair, and went into the utility room, then looked around and realized I'd forgotten why I went in there. Whenever my grandmother did that, she laughed and said she had too much on her mind.

So did I.

Muttering to myself, I slipped out the front door and got into my car.

I did want to visit my grandparents, of course, but I felt compelled to stop by Hamish's office. He had been caught up in our bizarre drama through no fault of his own, and I felt horrible that he'd been terrified by an orb. I also wanted to ask him about the researcher who had invented living metal. Hamish had completed his postgraduate work at the University of Edinburgh while the other man worked at the University of Glasgow, but Scotland wasn't a huge country. Had they ever met?

I spotted Hamish's convertible in the parking lot, and

the Gumby on the dash. Smiling, I slung my purse over my shoulder and knocked three times on the office door, then stepped into the waiting area. "Hamish?" I called. "Got a minute? It's Andi."

"Andi!" He came out of his office, both hands extended as though he were greeting a friend. "How are you feeling today?"

"Great, thanks to you. I wanted to stop by to thank you for—"

"Come in, come in," he said, ushering me into the inner office. "Have a seat while I make you some tea."

"I've just had breakfast—"

"No matter. A spot of tea always gets the day off to a good start."

What could I say? The man was Scottish. While he fussed at the coffee maker, I looked at his window. The curtains had been pushed aside, and both windowpanes were whole and clean. "Your window," I said. "Repaired already?"

"I couldn't leave it overnight," he said, turning toward me as the machine gurgled. "After all, these aren't my books on these shelves, and I'd hate for anything to go missing while I was renting the space. Thank heaven for 1-800-GET-GLAS."

He brought over two mugs and gave one to me. "Thank you," I said. "I seem to be saying that a lot, but I mean it. I was a little lost until I began meeting with you. I don't know what you did, but I can't thank you enough."

"I wish all my patients were as quickly mended." He sank into his chair. "You were—are—a delight."

I sipped from my mug, then frowned when my phone buzzed within the depths of my purse.

"Do you need to get that?" Hamish asked. "Might be important."

I glanced at the caller ID. "It's Brenda. We're leaving soon, so she probably wants to know if I've seen her shoes or something."

"Where are you going?"

"We're not sure. This work we do . . . is often spontaneous. We go where the tickets take us."

"Rather unnatural way to live. And who sends the tickets?"

I shrugged and let my head tip to the side, where it could rest against the side of the chair. "I don't know, and this gig is definitely better than being bored. Which reminds me—I am really sorry about the orb in your office. I don't know where it came from and I hope you never see another one." My voice sounded distant, and the room appeared to be filling with a slight haze.

"I have enjoyed getting to know you," Hamish was saying, "and Mother enjoyed meeting you, too. It's too bad we won't see you anymore. Mother greatly admired your thoroughness. She said your journals were the most interesting she'd ever read."

I blinked and tried to raise my head, only to find that it weighed about thirty pounds. "How ridiculous," I said, laughing as my nose nestled into the seam of the chair. "I can't seem to lift my head."

"It's the sedative," Hamish answered, and though I couldn't see him, I heard the subtle swish of his shoes over the carpet. He was moving about the room, doing something . . .

"Hamish?" I asked, struggling to lift my heavy eyelids. "Are you still there?"

The phone in my purse buzzed again and again and again . . .

Slowly, the fog in my head cleared. I opened my eyes and saw that I was still in the chair, but my hands had been tied together. Hamish was not sitting next to me, but leaning on the desk, an expectant expression on his face.

"Andi?" He lifted a brow. "Are you back, then?"

My mouth was as dry as cotton. "I'm . . . here."

He smiled. "Good. Have a few last minute details to arrange and I have to collect that orb from you. Can't have that roaming around, can we?"

"What . . . orb?"

"The one in that beach bag you call a purse."

I pressed my tongue to my teeth, trying to force the word over my clumsy tongue. "Th—there's no orb."

"I believe there is. So excuse me while I plunder your purse."

I watched in dazed astonishment as he picked up my bag and pulled out my phone. "Ah," he said, reading the screen. "Bjorn, Brenda, and the Professor have called several times in the last quarter hour. I trust you didn't tell them you were coming here?"

I blinked. What had I told them?

Hamish pulled up the orb, which had filled out the bottom of my large bag. "There." He smiled at the thing as it hummed and hovered a few centimeters above his open hands. "They will be pleased to know this little one has come home."

"Wh-who is—who are—?"

"You needn't worry about that, Andi. Thanks to your faithfulness, we now know everything your little group knows, and we can better plan for the future. You were so dutiful, obeying every hypnotic prompt, sending your neat little reports, keeping us in the loop—good girl. And now, I believe it's time to wrap things up and send you off."

"Wh-where?"

"It's all been arranged. I'm going to put you in your car and give you the trigger word, and then you will drive to the spot I have selected. You'll be the first to die, but you'll go peacefully, your conscious mind soundly asleep. Afterward, traces of a sedative in your blood will lead many to believe you were suicidal. Over the next few weeks, the others will meet with accidents, too—the professor is next in line. Due to his advanced age and fondness for you, no one will be surprised when he has a heart attack. The big oaf will follow—probably in a drunken brawl or some such thing. Then the artist, an easy job because tattoo parlors are *so* seedy, and the clientele not the finest. I believe she'll be robbed of whatever is in her cash box, just to keep things real. Without you lot to take care of him, the boy will be sent back to the hospital, where no one will mind anything he says."

Moment by moment, my mind cleared. This was no exercise; he was serious. He was one of them. And he was planning to kill me.

"I think that's about it." Hamish looked around his office and absently patted his pocket until he heard the jangle of keys, then he knelt in front of me. "Are you ready to go under?"

"You can't." I summoned every ounce of energy to glare into his eyes. "You can't make someone do what they don't want to do, even under hypnosis."

"Ah." His smile went soft and buttery. "But that's the thing, Andi—you were so upset over your recent illness that you wanted to die. You thought you were useless, that your splendid mind had gone to mush and your gifts had vanished. For days now, your subconscious has been ready to throw in the towel."

"But—"

"All we have time for, love. Say good-bye now." His smile vanished. "On the count of five, you will again fall into a deep and dreamless sleep. One . . . two . . . three . . . four . . . five.

I dreamed Hamish and I were walking along a dock, then Hamish gestured to a boat, opened a hatch, and waited until I climbed in. Then he went around, walking on water, and climbed into the opposite seat.

"Can't get used to riding on the right side," he said. "You mustn't drive without a seat belt, love. Put it on, please."

I did. As if they had a mind of their own, my fingers pulled the seat belt across my chest, then snapped it into place at my hip.

"Perfect," Hamish said, turning sideways to smile at me. "Let's go. Pull out into traffic and drive toward your grandparents' house."

I drove the boat, obeying traffic signs and signals and watching other boats zoom past as I held to the speed limit. "You're an exceptionally careful driver," Hamish said. "No one would believe that you drove into a retention pond accidentally, so it has to be suicide. Sorry about that. A bit hard on the reputation, I know, but you'll be past minding."

We drove into a very busy channel, and I maintained a steady speed in the right lane until Hamish pointed to an buoy. "This ramp, love."

I took it. "Now," he said, "pull onto the verge, the shoulder."

I pulled over, coasting until Hamish told me to stop. "Now," he said, smiling, "I'm going to get out. When the door closes you're going to accelerate and drive toward that pond over there. The ride might be a bit choppy, but you will hold the wheel steady. You'll steer straight toward the pond, and you'll remain calm as the vehicle fills with water because your struggle is finally over. Your friends will be better off without you, so go ahead, close your eyes, and sleep."

Then, while I stared at the world beyond the windshield, Hamish leaned forward, turned my face toward him, and kissed me for a long moment.

"Pity," he said, pulling away. "Such a waste."

I sat motionless, waiting, until I heard a door click. Then I pressed my foot to the accelerator and heard the responsive roar of the engines.

I heard the trickle of water and felt the boat slide on

the surface. So pleasant. I loved sleeping to the sounds of water.

MEGADEATH APPROACHING, CAPTAIN. DEFEND YOUR BATTLESHIP.

I blinked as sirens and horns disturbed my liquid lullaby.

MEGADEATH APPROACHING, CAPTAIN. DEFEND YOUR BATTLESHIP.

I shook my head as reality intruded into my fictive dream. I wasn't in a boat; I was strapped into my car. Water wasn't trickling nearby, it was pouring in through the doors, rising from the floor, and rushing up the windshield. The front end of my car had already gone under, and water was crawling up the car doors, covering my seat, drowning my purse.

My phone! I reached for it reflexively, but it had already gone silent beneath the murky water. I had to get out. I had to get *free*. I reached for the seatbelt buckle, my fingers frantically searching for the locking mechanism until I found it. I threw off the belt and tried to work the door handle, but the onrushing water seemed determined to hold the door closed. I could feel pressure squeezing my eardrums. The power window button wouldn't work, and I didn't have a hammer . . .

Water crept up my chest and tickled my neck. I snatched a deep breath and turned to kick at the window, but the steering wheel cramped my movements, leaving me little room to maneuver. The rising water was at my chin, filling my ears, so I tipped my head back, gulping air near the ceiling light. The car tilted, the driver's window plunged downward or maybe upward because I could no longer tell which way was up and which down.

I kicked, hit the fabric of the ceiling, and realized it, too, was soaked and there was no more air . . .

Oh, God, please . . .

As my eyelids fluttered at the bright light, I looked out and saw Tank bending over me with wide blue sky behind him. My gorge rose, and Brenda rolled me over while I vomited water and coughed liquid from my lungs. Then I was lying flat again, mud beneath my palms, wet clothes chilling my skin.

Four concerned faces peered at me from above—Tank, Brenda, Daniel, and the professor. When I blinked and asked why I was wet, four faces broke into wide smiles and the professor patted Tank on the back.

"I never thought guys like you could swim," the professor said. "I thought you'd sink like a stone. But you did it, my boy, you did it."

"Couldn't have done a thing without Brenda," Tank said, patting his pocket. His smile faded for an instant. "Oh—sorry. Must have dropped it in the pond."

Brenda waved his comment away. "Forget it. Aunt Rene will send me another Life Hammer once I tell her that you saved Andi's life with the first one. Maybe she'll send two."

I listened to them, more confused with each word. "Can I sit up?" I asked as sirens began to wail in the distance. "Is Daniel playing that game?"

"I think you should lie still," Tank said, placing a hand on my shoulder. "At least until the EMTs have a chance to look you over."

I blinked when I saw Daniel crouching next to Brenda. He wasn't holding his phone, so the sirens must be real . . .

Within a few minutes an ambulance had pulled up and a pair of young men lifted me onto a gurney. When the professor told them that I'd been pulled from a submerged vehicle and revived with CPR, the medics said I'd have to go to the hospital.

"Possibility of infection inside the lungs," one man said, pulling up the gurney's guardrail. "We won't release her until we're sure she's okay."

I would have protested, but at that moment I didn't

feel like the sharpest tack on the bulletin board. Maybe a few hours in the hospital would do me good.

Chapter 10

By the next morning, I'd had time to think about a lot of things. Lying in the soft light of a dim hospital lamp, I realized that a few days ago, all I'd wanted was to feel normal again. Because he was smart and handsome and charming, I trusted Hamish Drummond, even allowing him to hypnotize me.

I should have known better. I should have listened to Tank and Daniel. Because I didn't, Hamish had full access to my team . . . and now we were all in danger.

Would they ever forgive me?

I sat up and propped my elbows on the rolling bedside table. In the car, in that moment before I filled my lungs with water, I had called on God . . . and I was still alive. I wasn't exactly sure how or *if* He worked things out, but I was still alive and I didn't deserve to be.

I would never again let my heart overrule my head.

My friends showed up after breakfast. The professor greeted me with a vase of flowers and a printed sheet of paper. "The flowers are gorgeous," I said, burying my face in the fragrant carnations. "And what's that other thing?"

"Our next gig." The professor handed me an itinerary. "Day after tomorrow we're leaving for San Diego. So if you can refrain from getting into trouble—"

"Hush up, you ol' curmudgeon." Brenda sat on the edge of the bed, blocking my view of the professor. "Girlfriend, that one was too close for comfort. You gotta be more careful."

"I know. And I'm sorry for getting us into this mess."

Brenda patted my hand. "We're all still here, ain't we?"

"I'm still not sure what happened. I remember sitting in Dr. Drummond's office and hearing that I was about to die. Next thing I knew, I was in the car hearing the Megadeath battle cry. I think—I *know*—that sound snapped me out of my trance. But I couldn't get out in time." Even now, the memory of that chilly black water made me shudder. "Can you fill in the gaps for me?"

Brenda glanced at Tank and the professor, then she draped her arm around Daniel's shoulders. "Daniel-my-man, why don't you ask Tank to go get you some ice cream? I think there's a little shop down in the lobby area."

Tank stared at her. "Ice cream? In the morning?"

"Be a prince and take Daniel for a cone, okay?"

I watched silently as Daniel walked over to Tank, took his hand, and led the big guy through the doorway. When they were safely away, Brenda leaned forward. "I don't want to embarrass the kid. But we wouldn't have found you if not for him."

"Daniel?"

"Quite right." The professor leaned against the end of my hospital bed. "Once again I found myself grateful we had the boy along."

Brenda tossed the professor a disdainful look, then patted my hand again. "You'd gone out that morning. I don't think we even realized it, but suddenly Daniel had one of his episodes." She gave me a pained smile. "He started screaming about the duchs, and how they were all around you. We looked for you, of course, 'cause we wanted to show him that you were fine, then we saw your car was gone. I remembered you sayin' something about going to see your grandparents, but as soon as I mentioned that, Daniel started screamin' even worse, hollerin' and hittin' us if we got close. Then Tank opened the front door, and suddenly Daniel ran out and jumped in the rental car. Well, what else could we do? We got in, too, and then—" She paused to draw a deep breath. "You know how he has this invisible friend?"

I nodded.

"Since we didn't have a clue where you were, we went wherever Daniel told us to go. When he took us to the interstate I was convinced we were on some kind of wild goose chase, and then suddenly he pulls out his phone and starts playing *Battleship Megadeath*—the game he's got goin' with you. Then we're at the side of the road, and Daniel points to a pond. We're staring at it, and we see this huge air bubble come to the surface. Daniel freaks out again, jumpin' up and down, and Tank is ready to dive in, but before he can kick off his shoes Daniel reaches into my purse, pulls out that silly orange hammer, and hands it to Tank."

Brenda paused and drew a deep breath. "About that time, I was putting pieces together, and I didn't like what I was thinking. I had to take a CPR class to get my state license, and I *know* how fast a car can sink. Unless you can get your seatbelt off and your window down before the power shorts out, you're done for."

"I did get my seatbelt off," I said, shivering. "Barely."

Brenda shook her head. "Man, I get wore out just

thinkin' about it. But I'm sure you can figure out the rest. Out in the pond, Tank sees your car, breaks the window with the hammer, and pulls you out. If the water had been a couple of feet deeper, or if you'd still been stuck in that seat belt, I don't think Tank could have done it—the guy's got a lot of heart, but he's not what you'd call naturally buoyant. Anyway, Daniel stops screamin' once he sees that Tank has you, and he's as quiet as a mouse while Tank is givin' you mouth to mouth." She grinned. "Personally, I think he liked that even more than savin' your life. So that's what happened."

I leaned against my pillows, exhausted and a little amazed. The story made sense, but if I hadn't lived it, I wouldn't believe it.

"What about Hamish?" I shifted my gaze to the professor. "Has anyone checked out Dr. Drummond?"

"A couple of detectives went to talk to him," the professor said, "but he had vacated the premises—not a trace of him at the office, not even a fingerprint. But about an hour later the cops called me with news of a burning convertible on Interstate 275. The car sounded like Drummond's, so I went to the scene. No body, just a crumpled convertible on its side, resting in the middle of the median. And this." He pulled his phone from his pocket, tapped the photo icon, and let me see the screen. In a patch of charred grass, I saw Hamish's Gumby— twisted, melted, and an exact copy of Brenda's sketch.

"What does it mean?" I asked, lifting my gaze to meet the professor's. "Is he dead?"

The professor released a hollow laugh. "I wouldn't think so. But that's okay—neither are we."

I leaned back against the pillows and sighed as Tank and Daniel came back in. Tank carried a tray of ice cream cones, and as he passed them out I remembered Drummond telling me that all of us but Daniel were supposed to die, one after the other. But if the Gate couldn't manage to get rid of a defenseless girl like me, how powerful could they really be?

Maybe we'd soon find out.

"Thanks, Tank." I accepted a cone and tasted the vanilla on my tongue. Delicious.

SELECTED BOOKS BY ANGELA HUNT

Jamestown
Hartford
Rehoboth
Charles Towne
Magdalene
The Novelist
Uncharted
The Awakening
The Debt
The Elevator
The Face
Let Darkness Come
Unspoken
The Justice
The Note
The Immortal
The Truth Teller

The Silver Sword
The Golden Cross
The Velvet Shadow
The Emerald Isle
Dreamers
Brothers
Journey
Doesn't She Look Natural?
She Always Wore Red
She's In a Better Place
Five Miles South of Peculiar
The Fine Art of Insincerity
The Offering
Esther: Royal Beauty
Bathsheba: Reluctant Beauty
Delilah: Treacherous Beauty

Web page: www.angelahuntbooks.com

Facebook: https://www.facebook.com/angela.e.hunt

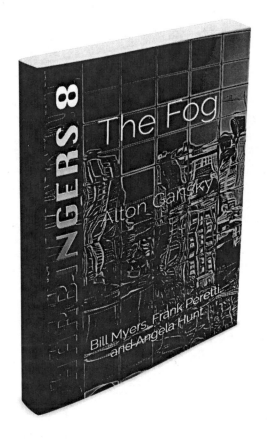

FROM HARBINGERS 8:

THE FOG

ALTON GANSKY

I know the people behind me are wondering what I'm doing. I can't blame them. It's not everyday you see a man my size standing on the parapet of a high-rise building in the middle of a major city and looking down at a street he can't see a mere fifty floors below. Did I mention it was night and the only light I have comes from emergency lamps? Probably not. I'm not at my best at the moment.

I've never admitted this to anyone before, but I don't like heights that much. I don't let on, of course. A big football player isn't supposed to have such fears. Well, I ain't a football player anymore. I'm just a big ex-jock teetering on the edge some five hundred feet above the sidewalk below.

It's eerie up here. Not just because most of the lights in the city are out but because of the silence. About a million-and-a-half people call San Diego home, or so the professor told me. He has a knack for such things. When we first arrived, I noticed the noise of downtown: traffic, people talking, busses, mass transit trains, and other noise-making things of humanity. Now all I can hear is the sound of a gentle breeze pushing at my back and zipping by my ears. That and the sobs of my friends behind me.

If all of that wasn't enough to raise the hair on a man's neck, there was the fog—a fog like I've never seen before. At first it looked like your garden variety fog, but if moved differently, and—how do I say this—it was populated.

Things lived in it. Bad things. Horrible things. Ugly things.

When I look down I can't see the street, just the roof of the fog bank. That and the things swimming in it.

A face appeared.

I shuddered.

It wasn't alone.

The things swam in the fog like dolphins swim in the ocean. Except dolphins are cute. These are no dolphins. No siree. These things ain't from around here. There not from anywhere on this earth. I can only guess where they call home, but if it was Hell, I'd believe it with no hesitation.

"Tank . . ."

Even with my back to her, I recognize Andi's voice. I would recognize it anywhere and anytime. The biggest hurricane couldn't keep her words from my ears.

I raised a hand. I didn't want to hear it. I wanted to hear it more than anything I've ever wanted. I know it doesn't make much sense, but I'm a guy standing on the edge of certain death, so my thinking, such as it is, has a few hiccups. Don't expect me to make a lot of sense at the moment. You stand on the edge of a high-rise an inch from death and see how well the gears in your head work.

I allowed myself one last glance back. I turned slowly to look at my friends and the scores of people standing behind them. I was real careful. When I go over the edge, I want it to be my decision, not a fool mistake.

My gaze first fell on Professor McKinney, worldwide lecturer, atheist, and former Catholic priest. Yep, he's a bit conflicted. He's the smartest man I've ever met, and at times, the biggest pain in my fanny. He is retirement age but hasn't slowed down. Good thing. The team needed him. He stared at me through his glasses. Even in the dim light provided by a pale ivory moon overhead and the emergency lighting, I saw something I had never seen before: a tear in his eye.

The professor's hand rested on Andi Goldstein's

shoulder. I let my gaze linger on her. My gaze always lingered on her. Her wild red hair might strike some as a bit strange, but she was fashion-model beautiful to me. There were tears running down her face. The sight of them squeezed my heart like a man might squeeze a lemon.

Next to her stood Brenda Barnick. Her black face seldom showed a smile and she could put on an expression that would melt steel. I've faced a lot of big guys on the football field, but not one of them put any fear in me. When Brenda lost her temper she plain scared me and anyone else within the sound of her voice. She's a street smart tattoo artist, all hard on the outside, but I know she has a great big heart. She looked away but not before I saw the fear and pain on her face.

One way I know Brenda has a big heart is the boy standing in front of her. The kid has mental problems. Well, that's what the doctors say, but we know better. He's just different. And talented. Brenda, through a lie or two, got herself named his guardian. She makes a good mom.

The sight of my friends gutted me. I turned from them. It was easier looking at what I feared rather than those I love. I was on this ledge for them and for many others.

I raised my right foot and inched it over the edge of the parapet. The breeze pushed at me as if encouraging me to jump.

The things in the fog were agitated, like sharks in bloody water. There small, lethal heads bobbed up and down in the fog.

They were waiting.

Waiting for me to lean forward.

I did.

A hundred pairs of clawed hands reached for me.

But first, I need to tell you how I got here.

Don't miss the other books in the Harbingers series:

Invitation, the first four volumes in one book!

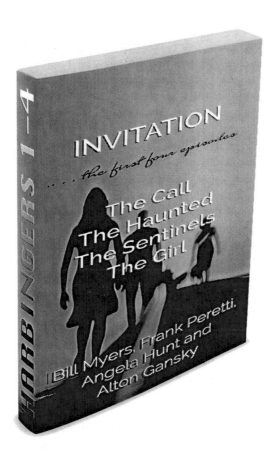

The Revealing, **by Bill Myers**

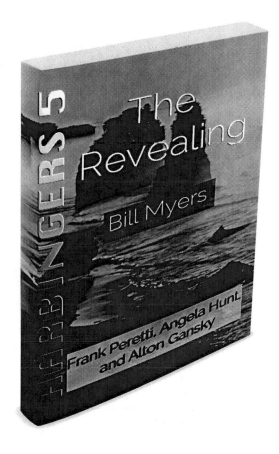

CPSIA information can be obtained at www.ICGtesting.com
Printed in the USA
LVOW10s2158240816

501735LV00014B/287/P